Bears in the Hibiscus

Janelle Meraz Hooper

Other books by the author:

A Three-Turtle Summer, novel
As Brown As I Want: The Indianhead Diaries, novel
Custer and His Naked Ladies, novel
Free Pecan Pie and Other Chick Stories, mixed genre

Be good and you will be lonesome.
• Mark Twain

To my family,
None of whom are represented in this book.
I promise.

$\mathscr{C}\!ontents$

1

Harvest Joy

When Mary's husband, Brian, decided to end their marriage, it didn't take him long to pack. That was because he had already been leaving, piece by piece, for years. Most of his clothes were already on the yacht that belonged to his father's timber company. He had never been the outdoorsy type, so they had no closets filled with tents and blue-speckled coffeepots to sort through like some divorcing Northwest couples did.

When the end finally came, she didn't cry a tear; all she felt was relief. As he rushed from room to room, opening closets and cupboards to make sure he hadn't forgotten anything, Mary searched for memorable parting words to mark the occasion. She found none. The best she could think of was a few hand gestures that she managed, with great effort, to keep to herself.

The adjustment was hard for Mary and her daughter, Kate. Almost overnight, everything changed for them. Their income, family status, and lifestyle made radical changes. Nearly two years later, the two were comfortable on their own.

Now, it was a Sunday morning, and Mary was on her deck. The sun didn't have any real warmth to it yet, but the air was fresh and lightly scented with the fragrance of spring.

No longer a stay-at-home wife, she savored her days off, even though she considered herself incredibly lucky to get a job in a literary field at her age. She still didn't know what made the publisher hire her. She'd never used her degree in journalism, and the world was full of writers. Almost all of them were younger and more qualified. It had to be that they were both single mothers trying to survive in a new world that had, without notice, changed the rules about men going to work and women staying home to raise their kids, prune the camellias, and make the meatloaf.

At least, the timing was good. Her daughter, Kate, was in high school now, and Mary had baked her share of cookies for the PTA, served on the county's charity boards, and worked on the state's political campaigns. She was bored, and ready for some new challenges. Ready, but unprepared. Although logic should have told her that her marriage would end someday, she hadn't made any preparations for joining the workforce. Divorce found her with a closet lacking anything that could be even loosely called office wear, her nails a wreck from the camellias, and hair that hadn't seen a good cut since she'd found a coupon in the library parking lot one rainy day.

Oh. And she was an emotional wreck that, for some reason, she was unable to overcome or hide. Other newly divorced women managed to put on a perky face, bravely go to the next singles' party, and flirt until they dropped. Why couldn't *she*? Twice, for days, she'd planned outfits to wear to singles' events she'd seen advertised in the paper. When she got there, she looked around at the men oozing with so much confidence they hadn't even bothered to change out of their faded polo shirts and wrinkled khaki pants. Each time, she'd made a quick break for the parking lot. She was not that needy. She would *never* be that needy. She'd become a nun first.

It had been a shock to be single again, and realize just how little her stock was worth in the dating market, now that she was no longer in her twenties. Once reality had set in, she was no longer surprised or hurt when her phone didn't ring on Saturday night. She had become like the big moon snails on the beach at Hood Canal. Still soft on the inside, but tough as a geode on the outside.

With a clear idea of what was likely, and what was not, she was finally moving on with her life.

Stretched out in the old plastic lounge chair on her deck, Mary forced herself to start a whole new train of thought. She closed her eyes to daydream about the imaginary man du jour. She had a lot of them. Some were serious. Some were funny. Some were short. Some were tall. But they all had one thing in common: they all adored her.

Today's imaginary man was one of the best so far. They were on a yacht on Puget Sound on a starry night. Mary snuggled into her chair and imagined him. Thin, late fortyish, and bright. She imagined she could smell his cologne. His closeness was electric as he sat beside her on some cushions on the deck and handed her a glass of wine. Together they gazed at the stars. She smiled. In her mind, it was easy to create a perfect world with no nastiness, no late child-support checks, no ex-husband, and no intimidating in-laws.

This gorgeous, literate man was nuzzling her neck and the side of her face. Mary could feel the gentle bobbing of the boat beneath them. "I want to make love to you," he whispered. Feeling no resistance, he pulled the cushions off the bench seats and made a comfortable spot for the two of them on the floor of the yacht and cradled Mary in his arms. He kissed her long and slow on the mouth and ran his fingers through her hair. His hand moved down her neck and easily found her breasts. Eagerly, he slipped his hand underneath her bottom as he pulled one of his legs over hers. When she felt the warmth of his soft laughter on the back of her neck, she was surprised. Before she could ask him what he found that was amusing, he rolled over and looked at the starry sky, took a deep breath of night sea air and said, "You know, I got a bigger boat than I needed for one person just so I'd have comfortable sleeping quarters on board."

"Is that funny?" Mary asked.

"No," he said, "what's funny is we're sprawled out on the deck like teenagers...let's go below..."

"I kind of like it here."

"Me, too, but there's not as much privacy on the deck as you might think. We're close to the traffic channel and the bigger vessels passing us have a clear view of us snuggled up on our cushions. Besides, I bought matching sheets and everything," he said playfully. He pulled himself up off of the deck and headed toward the cabin. "I'll turn down the bed and you join me when you're ready. Then he winked at her and added, "If you dare...I plan to have my way with you!"

The mood was broken when the dog next door started howling at a siren on a fire truck blocks away. Mary pulled herself up in her chair and pulled her sun hat down over her forehead. *Oh, what was the use? So she was lonely. What else was new?* At times like this, she forced herself to remember that she had been alone for years *before* her divorce. Days and weeks went by when she barely saw her husband. Even when he was home, it was only physically. His mind was off someplace else. At family events, Brian's absences raised his parents' eyebrows. Mary made excuses for him but she, too, wondered what he was up to. Was he really working? She suspected not, but there was no way to prove it, short of hiring a private detective. Snooping on people wasn't her style, so the loneliness and suspicion seeped into her life, like the mold that worked its way into cracks in her bathroom tile. She much preferred the loneliness she was experiencing now that she was divorced. It was a more honest kind of alone, and it didn't hurt nearly as much as when she was married and her empty bed refused to answer her question, "Where is he tonight? Who is he with?"

She reached for her coffee cup. It was empty. *Great. No sex. No coffee. What's next, world chaos? No wait, we already have that,* she reminded herself.

Okay, so Day 720 of celibacy for me. Give or take a month. Was this how Mother Teresa got her start? Mary breathed a wistful sigh and resigned herself to a day that would be minus any gorgeous man who'd gone to the trouble of purchasing matching sheets and pillowcases so he could have his way with her. According to a magazine article she'd recently read, the chances of her ever finding another man to love her was dwindling with each passing year. According to the article, they reached their conclusion by taking the number of eligible men, and subtracting the ones that were unsuitable:

The old.

The mentally unstable.

The gay.

The men totally unsuited to ever live with another woman due to the close proximity of other female influences (mama's boys).

That left only a handful of eligible men suitable for a woman in her late thirties, and they were dating women in their twenties. *Why? Because they could.* That left older men. *Much* older men. Somehow, Mary wasn't enthusiastic about beginning a relationship with a man who already had three ex-wives and five or six grown kids—all of whom would instantly hate her because she'd be viewed as a threat to their inheritance. Or, maybe, they wouldn't like the idea of someone replacing their mother. Her friends, who were dating older men, had told her all about it. It wasn't a pretty story.

She looked at her medium frame in the bathroom and didn't bother to take inventory of her many assets to boost her spirits as she sometimes did. Instead, she thought, *I'm a nice person. If no man wants me, screw him.* She no longer needed a man to be complete. She could use the free time to write a great American novel, join the Peace Corps, or learn to play the piano. She had absolutely no musical talent, so learning to play should occupy her until she was well into her eighties.

She didn't consider throwing herself into her work because she was already doing that.

So, what should she do today? She wondered as she reluctantly left her deck chair and went inside. Her weekend time was limited, and she had to make the best of her free Sundays. Mary did a quick mental check of her assets that would have to last until the end of the month. She had eighty dollars in her checking, and nothing in savings unless she counted the change in the Wonder Woman cookie jar her friend, Roxanne, had given her for her birthday. The library was looking like a good, fiscally responsible place to spend the day.

Was Kate up yet? The quiet on the other side of the door could mean that she was studying in bed, or that she was still asleep. Well, let her sleep. A few more months and she'd be out of high school, and she'd have to find a part-time job. Then, after college, she'd be working the rest of her life. Finally, Mary had learned that times had changed. Women would no longer be able to stay home, raise children, and put away pickles while the husband worked at a fulltime job. *We have been liberated. Now we get to clean house, cook meals, take care of the kids, and work a forty-hour week. The Good Ship Lollipop had sailed without them.* Mary had loved staying home to raise Kate, but now she asked herself, *what was she thinking? How had it never occurred to her that she needed to build wealth of her own for the future?*

Apparently, she was one of the last to understand the concept of financial security. A few years ago, when all of her neighbors went back to work and left her to run the neighborhood's first non-profit daycare, why didn't she get the message? Now, the few men she did meet asked her four questions before the foam was off the latte: "Where do you work?" "How much do you make?" "What kind of car do you drive?" And, "Do you own your own home?" Mary quickly caught on that, in a community property state, a lot of men were more interested in recouping the money they'd lost in their past divorces than they were in romance. She didn't know how much she'd have to make, and how big her house would have to be before she'd find a man to adore her like the ones in her fantasies, and she wasn't interested in finding out.

While Mary straightened her bed, she caught sight of a little handmade sign she'd put on her night table. It simply said: "Harvest Joy". The sign was meant to remind her that she had a life too. And now, it was up to her to put the joy back into it. She could no longer hold her breath and wait for her husband to take a few minutes from his busy schedule to brighten her day. Lots of times, she felt she was the only one who was alone. Wherever she went, she saw relaxed couples shopping together or taking advantage of an unexpected sun break to stroll along the waterfront in the middle of the week. Once, she was so frustrated about being alone on a beautiful day that she struck up a conversation with a couple that was strolling in her direction.

"Tell me," she asked, jokingly, "how is it you have time to take your wife for a walk on the beach in the middle of the week?"

The man answered with a smile, "Life is short." His wife leaned into him and hugged his arm. Somewhere, Mary knew, they were still out there, strolling and drinking gourmet coffee from heavy, cardboard cups with custom paper sleeves. How she envied them.

And where was she? Alone. Drinking coffee that would never be sold in a fancy, paper cup. *What to do?* She picked up the phone and called her best friend, Roxanne. Last night, the crazy redhead had called her at eleven o'clock to say she was in bed with two men, Ben & Jerry. Newly divorced, and with an empty nest she, too, was picking up her life where she'd left off. Roxanne told Mary that she'd married her high school sweetheart the summer after they'd graduated.

By the time they divorced twenty years later, there was nothing of her left. The last time she'd seen the real Roxanne was sometime in the summer between high school and college. She missed her. She wanted her back.

"Are you up? Have Ben & Jerry left yet?"

"Oh, my God, I fell asleep," Roxanne answered, "they're here under the bedcovers somewhere!"

"Roxanne!"

"No, it's all right, here's the spoon and empty carton. Ben & Jerry are gone."

"Boy are you lucky. By now you could have Ben & Jerry running all over your new bed set. But then, this would be the week to need new bed linens. Our favorite department store is having a $79.00 bed-in-a-bag sale."

"I've got the bed in a bag," Roxanne murmured, "let me know when they have a man-in-the-bag sale."

"I'll keep a sharp eye on the ads."

"What's up?"

"I have to go to the library. Want to go with me and stop for coffee?"

"Let's stop at Gus's and have coffee and breakfast."

"Poor Ben and Jerry. How quickly they're forgotten."

Roxanne ignored her friend. "Let's go before ten, we can get in on the special."

"Cholesterol at an affordable price! I like it. Can you get dressed and meet me there before the special prices end?"

"If I'm not there, order a special for me. Two eggs over easy, bacon, with dry toast."

"Trying to make up for last night, huh?"

"Not really, I'm just not sure what tub of processed toxins Gus's is substituting for their margarine these days. Did you see my bread last Sunday? It had a blue scum on it."

"Haven't you heard? Gus's is going green. Now their butter is half real butter and half olive oil."

"Do I barf now or later?" Roxanne asked. Before she hung up, she said, "And, Mary, don't bother to bring your books. It's Sunday. The library is closed."

"Drat. I need something to read."

"Amazon delivers."

"And so does Visa. I'm going to let my tax dollars pay for my books this month."

Mary turned and saw a petite teenager wearing a University of Puget Sound sleep shirt a friend had given her. "Where are you going?" her daughter asked.

"Gus's. Want to go?"

"Does Gus have organic yogurt and Grape-Nuts?"

"No, but he has eggs from free-range chickens and green, wholesome pancakes."

"Thanks, but I'll pass. His food isn't green because it's healthy. You keep eating that stuff and they'll make you turn in your Splendor card."

"Why?"

"Because Splendor likes us to be slim so we make their clothes look good."

"I'll go to Bundle's, then. They'll love me even if I have to wrap myself in one of their bed sheets. Besides, I no longer bow towards Splendor every morning during prayers."

"Since when?"

"Since they cut my card into a million pieces right in the middle of the shoe department!"

"Well, that was just plain rude," Kate chuckled. She and her mother had hit many bumps in the road during the last two years; most of them had been met head-on with humor.

On the refrigerator's door, Mary kept the postcards that her ex sent their daughter from Hawaii, the Caribbean, Mexico, and other exotic spots. They were there partly because Kate wanted them there, but also to remind Mary that she'd been used, and that she had to come out on top. Somehow. It was pretty scary being left with no retirement, no job training, and no savings. The divorce settlement left her the house that wasn't paid for, a car that had over a hundred thousand miles on it, and spousal support that had petered out months ago. In her nightmares, Mary saw herself waitressing like that eighty-two-year-old woman who advertised prescription pain-killers on television.

"Geez, Louise, next time," Roxanne had counseled, "get a meaner lawyer."

"I'm pretty sure there won't be a next time. I can't imagine any man being worth the trouble. My radical new financial plan is to learn to survive on my own nickel."

While Kate was still living at home, one of Mary's financial survival tactics was to harvest joy on less. Money does not in itself make a quality life, she'd decided. All right, it helped. But it wasn't the only ingredient.

She had learned this truth right after her divorce when she was walking in downtown Tacoma with Roxanne. The hill on 11th Avenue was steep and she was wearing high heels. She was glad for an excuse to rest when her friend stopped to say hello to a young man that she knew.

"Found a job yet, Bob?" Roxanne asked.

"No, and my unemployment is about to run out," the young man volunteered. "I hope I don't have to move back home!" he said with a laugh. "Besides, I think my mom has made a walk-in closet out of my old room."

This man was clean, had a light in his eyes, and wore neatly pressed clothes. Bright, articulate, and cheerful, he didn't at all fit Mary's vision of someone who was unemployed.

"What are you doing to keep busy?" asked Roxanne.

"Oh, I went to a free concert last night, and this afternoon I'm going to usher at the little theatre. I get to see the play free that way," Bob said.

Mary was impressed. That young man was the inspiration behind the *Harvest Joy* sign on her night table. There was definitely more than one path to happiness, and she was determined to find the best quality of life for her and her daughter that her income could provide.

She reintroduced both of them to the library card, and tossed the siren's call to book clubs into the garbage. Entertaining was scaled down from two or three courses to dishes like homemade soup and bread, meatloaf and baked potatoes, or tacos. Dessert was ice cream, or sometimes, fresh fruit from their apple and cherry trees. Pizza and a movie became pizza *or* a movie.

Mary was prepared to learn basic plumbing for broken sink pipes to save on plumbing bills, but luckily, Kate had boyfriends who were handy with hacksaws and wrenches, and she rarely started a project she had to finish. At first, she felt guilty, but she was grateful to learn they were more than glad to help. Kate, on the other hand, was devastated that her long hair that clogged the bathroom drain was now permanently burned into the memories of the boys she dated.

At first, their biggest problem was Kate's wardrobe. The clothes at Splendor were the clothing of choice in Kate's upscale social group, and they were way beyond what Mary could afford. Luckily, Kate hit upon her own style that didn't depend upon the latest trends. The savvy teen went classic, and built a wardrobe partially-centered around jeans, assorted university sweatshirts, and matching baseball caps that were perfect in the rainy Northwest. A jean jacket completed her new look. The style was soon copied by her friends, and Mary was sure she heard a deep sigh of relief from some of the other single parents in their group.

Other articles of clothing, like purses and shoes, were picked up at the local outlet stores. The motto, "Never pay retail" became a way of life for Kate and her other frugal friends whose parents were divorced. She also benefited from her father's passion for shopping, and often returned from weekends with him carrying a bagful of wardrobe treasures from the Splendor outlet stores. Whenever he brought Kate home after one of their shopping trips, Mary could see glimpses of the old Brian in his face, and it made her wistful for the good old days. She was glad Kate got to see her dad in such a happy, giving mood, and that their daughter was able to comfortably spend time with both of her parents.

For her back-to-work wardrobe, Mary didn't get away as easy, but she did discover three-piece suits at Bundles. She bought two of them and mixed or matched the jackets to the skirts and pants. It broke her heart to spend her limited funds on the shoe of choice at her new job: an expensive, flat, ugly sandal with cork soles and buckles that she'd refused to wear even when she was in college. She purchased one pair of the gaggers, as she called them, then tried not to look down.

The breakfast she was going to have with Roxanne was also a money-saver. To draw in early birds, the restaurant served a ninety-nine cent special on the weekends. No matter what color its eggs were, the price was right.

2

A piece of your floor

The breakfast crowd was thinning by the time Mary and Roxanne got to Gus's. Their window seat overlooked a four-lane road lined with garish neon billboards that advertised the local Indian casinos. Mary laughed while Roxanne casually collected the vases of plastic flowers from the surrounding unoccupied tables and lined them up on their windowsill to block out some of the view.

"I wish I was going with a man to Hawaii," Mary confided when the conversation turned to her upcoming vacation.

"Maybe you'll meet someone over there."

"Not likely. I'm past the age where men follow me down the beach panting. I'm afraid I'll spend the whole vacation looking over my shoulder for some guy who'll never be there. I won't be able to relax. If I had a man with me already, I wouldn't be looking behind every palm tree for romance. I could get some rest. I know it'll never happen. I just wish I could be a part of a couple with someone for a week. I wouldn't even care if he fell asleep every night on the lanai with a can of beer in his hand. Just so he was there."

The two became quiet as they contemplated reality. They weren't kids anymore. "I'll be closing in on forty in a few years," Mary continued, "no man around here, even if he is straight, is going to sweep me into his arms and take me to a tropical island." Mary stirred her coffee, and tried to brush off a feeling of sadness. "And even if there *were* someone one who was passable and interested in me, I don't need a man right now to complicate my life.

I can barely make it from payday to payday. I don't need romance; I need fiscal stability."

"If there was a guy who'd go with you to Hawaii, what would the sleeping arrangements be for this temporary relationship made in pineapple heaven?"

"It doesn't matter. It's all a fantasy, remember?"

"Why do you keep running away from sleep-ins? What have you got to lose?"

"The real question is, what have I got to *gain*? I don't have enough time or energy to make another mistake."

"The real *answer* is, we both know you're going to end up taking your daughter and watching her hormones jump on the beach for the whole seven days."

"I can't. She has summer school to bone up on math for college." Then to change the subject, she asked, "What are you doing for the rest of the day?"

"I'm going to see my mom, we're having a family dinner. The woman cooks like she's Wilma Flintstone. With any luck, I'll come home with enough leftovers to last me the whole week."

Mary's idea for a temporary companion for her approaching vacation was never mentioned again. It was never a serious idea, anyway. Before she knew it, she was out of time. She forced herself to pick up the phone and call the airline. She had to find out if the tickets she had leftover from a ski trip she'd never taken with Brian were still good and if she could change the destination to Hawaii. When her ex had moved out of the house, he'd left her ticket and taken his. He'd acted like he was giving her such a gift! Angry, she'd thrown the tickets in the bottom of her sock drawer. She was in no mood to wallow in snow. But she did have an idea about where he could put the ski poles.

The tickets were good, but the rules had changed, and Mary would have to pay a transfer fee. *Fine.* She booked a flight for June 21st. Return June 28th.

Did she require a special meal? *No.*

New regulations limited carry on baggage. *Fine.*

She may be searched for concealed weapons. *Even better. Would he be cute?*

The companion forgotten, she decided if she could talk Peg, in the advertising department, into letting her sell some ads she, at least, might not have to live on peanut butter and crackers for a week. She was pretty sure Peg would help her out. When she had first started with *Sea the Northwest*, she'd started out in sales. Her boss had stuck her there just to give her a job until the writing slot was available. When Mary left advertising to take the writing position, Peg had offered to give her some hours if she ever needed them.

Kate would stay with her grandparents. Her scheme to stay with a friend was out of the question. All of her friends were driving now. Worrying about where Kate was and what she was doing would make rest for Mary impossible and she might as well stay home.

After the important details were decided, Mary's plans sagged like an old cedar deck. Truth be told, she wasn't at all excited about a vacation alone. She'd barely looked at all of the travel brochures she'd collected. The one about Diamond Head interested her the least. Washington State had its own volcano a few years back. Why on earth would she want to travel thousands of miles to look at another one? Even the idea of seeing molten lava didn't appeal to her unless she had a stick and a marshmallow. Besides, the whole idea of a Hawaiian vacation had sprung from a list she'd made after Brian moved out. A lot of impossible things were on that list. Things like: date only intelligent men, get a new car, lose ten pounds, and take an exotic vacation. Although the idea of a vacation alone was unsettling, the trip to Hawaii was the most doable goal on her two-year-old list. Mary felt pressured, if only by herself, to check off at least one of the four. Besides, her tickets were non-refundable, so she was committed. She was going, even if that hotel she booked sank into the ocean and she had to sleep on a picnic table at the beach.

With that thought, she picked up the phone and called the advertising department. "Hey, Peg, got a minute? I want you to let me sell a few ads for some extra vacation money. Hawaii. Great. What have you got?" She groaned when she heard the loser account Peg threw to her. "Is that all you've got?" Mary pleaded. "They haven't bought an ad in months! Oh, well, give me the new info. If I can't sell this, can I try again with another?" Peg said she could. Mary was fairly certain that she'd need a second chance.

She looked at her notepad in disbelief: North Hill Pet Cemetery. *I may be going to Hawaii on the back of a dead dog. That is, if I'm luckier than the dog.* How was she going to get that old woman to buy an ad in an upscale magazine? Their magazine's readers never buried their beloved departed pets; they had them cremated and sprinkled their ashes off the sterns of their yachts.

Well, she was running out of time. She'd better make a cold call on the way home. If she could sell an ad, she wouldn't get paid until the ad department had the check. Even worse, some clients wouldn't pay until they saw the ad in print because magazines had a reputation of coming and going, usually overnight. The next issue, Spring/Summer, would be coming out the end of June. That wouldn't get her a check before she left, but as long as she knew the money was coming in, she could use credit cards in Hawaii.

Okay, she'd better finish that story about the woman who makes whole wheat fortune cookies as big as dinner plates in her kitchen and fills them with personalized, divorce messages for women. It was one of Mary's favorite stories. A few issues back, she'd done a story about another woman who made normal-sized fortune cookies and filled them with good wishes to be used as wedding favors. It amused Mary that, for a divorce, the message required a cookie the size of a dinner plate.

Then, she'd hit the freeway a little early. Her magazine only published twice a year, so she'd been able to keep up on all of her other assignments. The really rough week was when they put the magazine together and took it to the printer. Each time, they barely made the printer's deadline, partly due to an antiquated cut and paste assembly system, and partly to an inexperienced staff that was overworked and underpaid. Mary was aware that most magazines' productions were almost completely computerized, but she wasn't anxious for a technical update in their publishing system. Right now, they jobbed out the magazine blueline to an outside graphic firm and that suited her just fine. When she finished a story now and hit the "send' button, her work was done. An upgrade in their system might, somehow, increase her workload. With a high school senior in the household, she couldn't work any more hours than she was working now. She wanted to spend all the time she could with Kate before she left the nest. Besides, she was tired, and she couldn't give up on the idea of having a life someday, regardless of what the marriage market statistics said. As she sat back in her chair, she surveyed her ragged manicure. *Right. I'm ready to be wined and dined, all right. By whom, somebody really desperate?* It was a good thing she'd promised herself after her divorce that she wouldn't date again until Kate went away to college. By then, she should have a little extra income. *At least enough for a new bottle of nail polish, she smirked to herself.* Never, she vowed, would she ever again be in a position where finances were so tight.

She left work early and headed down Pacific Highway, taking a left at the Y that led to North Hill. Much too soon, she saw the neon sign with a little barking dog that had a halo swirling around and around his head. The lights in the office were still on. When she got out of her car, she looked around to take in a breathtaking view of Mt. Rainier. It would have been even prettier if it hadn't been the backdrop for a few hundred tombstones made out of granite-colored resin. *But the colorful, plastic flowers covering the little graves lined up like biscuits in a pan are a nice touch,* she noted as she found the path that led to the office door.

As soon as she entered the room, she was hit by the smell of two kinds of alcohol. The kind you clean up exam tables with, and the kind you drink. *Oh, no, please tell me this woman isn't drunk.* As Mary got closer, she could see Mildred was hunched over a little black and white television, watching the news.

"You the black lab that was caught in the bear trap?" Mildred asked without looking up.

"No, Mildred, it's me, Mary Bergstrom from *Sea the Northwest Magazine.* Do you remember me?"

"Sure," she said unconvincingly, "come on in. Want a drink?"

"No, thanks. You're working late tonight."

"Yeah, waiting for a black lab that got too curious. What can I do ya for?"

Mary took a breath and jumped in, "Well, I came to see if I can talk you out of some of your advertising budget."

"What magazine are you from again?"

"Sea the Northwest."

"Oh, of course, hon, how are ya?" Mary was surprised by the turnabout in the old lady. She turned off the TV, straightened up, seemed to sober up, and was ready for business. "Let me have a look-see at that price list. Have they gone up?"

"Not since I saw you last. A third of a page is still three fifty an issue."

"Has your circulation gone up any?"

Mary, embarrassed, said, "No, but it's been stable," she answered, as she'd been coached by the ad department.

"Well, it's been a rough year for all of us. We even started making our own tombstones. Did you like them?"

"Very nice. They look like real granite."

"Funny you should stop by. Been thinking about advertising our new services."

"The tombstones?"

"No, your yuppie readers will never bury their pets here. What I'm talking about is our new sperm freezing service." She saw the look of amazement on Mary's face, and explained, "It's the latest thing in the pet business around here. Of course, it's been in California for years. What we do is freeze the sperm of your animal so you can always have a litter from your beloved pet even if he gets run over by a car, or caught in a bear trap."

"Does it work?"

"Sure, it works. And yes," she said, anticipating her next question, "it's legal. You have a pet? Bring it over here and I'll show you how it's done."

"Thanks, but I don't have any pets. Is this procedure expensive?"

"Yes, and that's why your little yuppies will eat it up. Tell you what. I got absolutely no response from my ad in your magazine last time. But I'm willing to try it again if you'll give me a deal."

"I can give you a cut rate if you'll sign a two-year contract. That's four issues." Any good salesman would have pushed for a three or four year contract, but she didn't want to be greedy. Plus, Mildred had been drinking, Mary wondered if her sales pitch might be a teeny bit unethical. Mary suggested, "How about if you buy one third of a page, for one year, and I take off one hundred dollars, bringing it to six hundred dollars even?"

"How about I take one third of a page, for *two* years, and you knock off three hundred dollars?"

This lady isn't drunk. She can smell my desperation and she's out to clean up. Mildred was rummaging around in her desk drawer. She came up with a notebook full of checks and made much ado about putting the carbon behind the check and picking just the right pen from the German shepherd coffee cup on her desk.

"Well? Do we have a deal?" she asked, her pen poised over the empty check.

If ad sales weren't down, the ad department would never accept a deal like this, but Mary knew that the magazine needed the money. She pulled out a contract and said, "Done."

Halfway through writing the check, Mildred stopped and asked, "You gonna do the lay-out and provide the artwork?"

"Sure, Mildred, we can do that; I'll have the ad department call you for your instructions."

Mildred started to write again, then stopped again. "You're not going to put me in some god-awful spot in the back where nobody will see it, are you?"

This lady is good. Mary answered, "Mildred, ads are placed on a first-come, first-serve basis. But I'll get you the best position I can for this issue, and it can be even better for the next." Mildred nodded. Suddenly, Mary saw a change come over Mildred's face. The old broad smelled blood. "How about throwing in a story about my new sideline to go with the ads?" Mary looked at the woman, hoping she was kidding. She wasn't.

"I can't promise, but I'll have the editorial department call you." Mary had a feeling she would be writing a story on artificial insemination for the next issue. Lordy. How was she going to write the story Mildred wanted for a family magazine? It would be a challenge.

They saw headlights coming up the driveway. The cagey woman held out the check and said, "Here's my bear trap fatality. Thanks for coming by, hon."

Saved by a bear trap. Mary had the feeling that even Mildred had her doubts about getting her story in the magazine, because she didn't push for a commitment. When Mary turned to leave, the woman pointed to a pile of tee-shirts by the door with Mildred's Dog Heaven emblazoned on their fronts. The halo on the little dog was metallic, and the dog had some kind of a holographic finish that made it look like it was jumping up and down for joy. "Take a tee-shirt, hon. No charge. You can wear it to work."

"Thanks, Mildred." Mary snatched a shirt off the shelf and hurried to her car; she was an easy crier and didn't want to meet a stricken couple with a dead dog on the narrow path. Before reentering the highway, she looked down at the check on the seat next to her. Barely able to keep from doing a hula in the front seat, she pounded on her steering wheel and shouted, "Yes! Yes! Yes!"

* * *

The next day when Mary went to work, she felt better than she had for weeks. At last, her vacation plans were beginning to fall into place. Maybe she'd get a vacation after all. The little nagging doubts and fears that occasionally surfaced were quickly smothered by her mantra chanted over and over under her breath, "Harvest joy, harvest joy, harvest joy!"

"Line one, your ex-brother-in-law," the receptionist said. Brian only had one brother, so it wasn't necessary to ask which one.

"Mark! Where are you?"

"Here in Montana recovering from the last forest fire that almost killed all my critters."

"I know the fires have been bad this year. How are the kids, are the girls still with Linda?"

"Yeah, and they're fine. I had them for spring vacation. John saw *A River Runs Through It* at a neighbor's cabin and now he fancies himself a fly fisherman."

"Is he catching anything?"

"Not much, but he looks real good in his Nisqually rubber boots, twill pants, plaid shirt, and fly vest with the matching hat that has just the right angle on it."

"Sounds like *he's* the one who's been caught! Who's buying all this yuppie stuff, you or his mom?"

"He is. He got a job cleaning and repairing fishing cabins over near Glacier. Loves to talk about all the shallow New Yorkers and their new, expensive gear that, unlike *him*, they'll use just once before they get bored."

"How do you respond to that?" Mary laughed.

"I'm real quiet. I just put on my *Real men don't use worms* tee-shirt and do my same old catch and release thing."

"Is that the same tee-shirt I bought you when we were over there years ago?"

"Yep, it still has a lot of wear in it."

"I'm going to send you a Splendor catalog."

"Not me! Our local outfitter is still my kind of place, and they give away glassware with every tankful of gas."

It was good to hear from an old friend, even if he was a Bergstrom. Mary was in no hurry to end the conversation.

"So what are you doing for vacation?" she asked.

"I'm going to Hawaii to sleep in a state park with a bunch of other rangers. I met some of them at a conference in Arizona last summer; they seem like nice guys. What are you doing?"

"Oh, I'm doing the Hawaiian thing too, only I'm sleeping in a hotel with room service and chocolates on the pillow." She heard laughter on the other end of the line.

"When are you going?" he asked.

"I leave on the 21st of June. When do you leave?"

"I fly out of Sea-Tac on the 20ᵗʰ. That's why I'm calling. I want to borrow a piece of your floor the night before."

"We'd love to have you!"

"Are you sure? There's no big Kahuna in your life who'll be upset?"

"I wish! No, I'm working too hard to hop the bars, and all the eligible guys at work are gay."

"That's against the Bible!"

"Oh, yeah? Who was just telling me he's going to Hawaii to sleep on the beach with a bunch of park rangers wearing loin cloths?"

"Well, I was going to invite you down to the beach for a cook-out but, on second thought, maybe you'd just be in the way."

"Darn. Another opportunity lost. See why I don't have any dates?"

"Well, I better let you get back to work since it looks as though you're going to be your own sole source of support for some time to come."

"Okay, but we'll see you on the nineteenth. If you have any of those trout that you never got around to releasing, bring them! I haven't had wild trout since we were there last."

"I've got some. I keep a few to impress visiting rangers. See you guys soon, and thanks, sis."

"Oh, Mark, it's really our pleasure. Goodbye."

After she hung up, she grinned, *that'll keep the neighbors buzzing.* Then it hit her, *now* she was really committed. If she didn't go on vacation, it would get back to her ex. She couldn't take that. Well, now she was vacationing. Whether she *should* or not! Whether she could *afford* to or not! Whether she *wanted* to or not!

3
The Montana Kahuna

Mary was so busy getting her ducks in order so she could get out of town, she didn't have time, at first, to think much about Mark spending the night at her house. When she did, she wondered why had he picked *her* house, when he had a brother nearby? Actually, he had his *own* place a few miles away, on his parents' compound. Why was he spending the night on *her* floor?

Before she went to bed the night before his visit, she made sure he could *find* the floor. All of the old newspapers, newsletters and mail-ads were either banished to recycling or put into a box in her car trunk so she could take them to Ray, who ran the layout department. Other peoples' magazines were a gold mine for layout and design ideas, not to mention leads for new clients for the advertising department. Mary would almost sooner throw away money than old magazines.

A rental car was in the driveway when she got home the next night, and she had a rush of guilt for not offering to pick Mark up at the airport...*what was she thinking?*

She forgot her guilt when she got a whiff of something wonderful. Something only vaguely familiar. Something—trout! She raced upstairs, not sure which sight was more welcome, Mark or the trout he and Kate were cooking in the skillet.

"Mark! You brought the fish, I could have at least cooked them!"

"That's okay, sis," Mark grinned. "Kate wanted to learn how to cook fish that aren't named Charlie."

"It smells wonderful! I love the way you cook fish with just salt, pepper, and flour. I hate all those Frenchy sauces."

"When there's sauce on the trout, lookout!" Mark cautioned, "It's probably covering up a fish that's older than you are."

"I guess being frozen kept them fresh on the trip," she said as she admired the full skillet.

"Actually, I got up early and caught these before I left the park. You'd been without so long I figured you were due. Kept them cool in an old Styrofoam ice chest."

"Did you get any strange looks at the airport when you checked your fish box luggage?"

"No, the floor was covered with ice chests bigger than mine that belonged to people who had been fishing for kings in Alaska. My little chest looked kind of pitiful next to theirs."

"The best things come in small packages, they say."

Mary left the cheerful cooks to change into a boxy pair of khaki walking shorts and a forest green tank top. She had a closet full of similar clothes. Her outfit was fine for the Northwest, especially since she was having dinner with a Montana Ranger, but she had trouble picturing it on a Hawaiian beach. She'd have to dig deeper into her closet and see if she could find something a little brighter.

Before she returned to the kitchen, Mary gave herself a quick look in the mirror. What looked back at her was a woman with long brunette hair and a medium frame. She was a few pounds lighter than the last time Mark had seen her, and she'd lost her tan. Both changes could be attributed to an increased workload. She hadn't stopped any cars lately, but she thought she looked as well as she could without the benefit of one of those instant facelifts she kept reading about in the women's magazines.

How she hated being the ex-wife. What would this ex-brother-in-law say to Brian the next time they spoke? Maybe,

"I saw your ex, she looks pretty good for her age, but your new love is a real knockout." It distressed her to imagine other people commenting, "I saw your ex, she had wrinkles all over her face! No wonder you're shopping around for a trophy wife." Well, she doubted that people would actually make those comments out loud, but that didn't mean they wouldn't *think* them. Mary hated most to hear, "When I look at Kate, I can see just how pretty Mary must've looked *years ago*." Mary loved her daughter, and they did look a lot alike, but who could compete with someone half her age?

Well, she was hungry, and she doubted her two cooks would deliver fresh, pan-fried trout to her bedroom door. "There she is!" greeted Mark when Mary entered the kitchen, "How about some wine?"

"Oh, you must have found my cardboard box in the fridge," Mary said as she held out her glass.

"Yep. Park rangers know how to find their quarry. It was marked Wednesday, so I thought it must be fresh."

"Very funny. Actually, I've got a box dated Thursday, I'm giving you the old stuff."

"It tastes good to me."

Dinner was delicious. Mary looked down at a plate of fresh trout, green salad with raspberry dressing, and lightly buttered and toasted Como bread, and thought she was in heaven.

After Kate downed her trout like it was a burger at Dollar's and left with a carload of friends, Mary and Mark settled down with fresh glasses of wine on the sundeck. Mary cringed as a whole flock of fruit bats flew into her big cherry tree. The crows stripped her fruit trees in the daytime and this was the night shift. Not surprisingly, she preferred the crows.

"So, how's it going, sis?" Mark asked as he eased into a deck chair that had seen better days.

"Not bad. How about you?"

"Good. I'm really looking forward to getting away for a few days. I didn't get much rest this year after the forest fires started."

"Kate and I watched the news every night. It was the worst we'd ever seen."

"That's for sure. We were lucky we didn't lose any of the firefighters."

The niceties were over, and Mary asked what she really wanted to know, "Mark, you know you're welcome here, but why did you come here instead of the compound or your brother's?"

"Mom is letting company from Minnesota use my house at the compound while they're here on vacation. And I didn't feel up to spending the night staring at the bare chest of Brian's latest Seahawk cheerleader. I think he should start carding those girls. Besides," he said with a twinkle in his eye, "I thought it would be tacky to sleep on my brother's floor when I was thinking about dating his ex."

Mary choked on her wine, and reached for a tissue from her pocket before wine came out of her nose. "Mark! Don't go there!" Mary said with surprise.

"Too late! I've already bought a ticket! What's wrong? Have someone else?"

"No..."

"I have cooties?"

"No...Mark, I like you, but I'm just not sure if it's smart for me to get involved with a Bergstrom again. You're a great guy, but I don't think I fit in with the rest of your family."

"Mary, you fit in just fine. Don't be intimidated by the Bergstrom money. It has nothing to do with me or us."

Mary was still wiping wine from her nose when she said, "I can't help the way I feel."

"Well, I always like to leave a woman in a state of shock, so I'll go to bed now," he said with a grin. "Thanks for the hospitality, sis. I'll be gone when you wake up, so I'll call you in Hawaii to see if you've managed to get your mouth closed yet." Mary felt him hesitate as he walked behind her chair, but he kept walking. *Was he going to touch her? Pat her on the head? What?*

Whatever he almost did, Mary was glad he hadn't. Her brain was occupied trying to list all of the reasons why their dating wouldn't be a good idea. Mark had already left the sundeck, so whatever thoughts she had remained unspoken. She was left with an empty deck chair, half a glass of wine, and a big full moon that she was sure was laughing at her. Or was the laughter she heard coming from the bathroom where Mark was? She vaguely felt a mosquito chewing on her bare arm and swatted it with one hand while she finished her wine with the other. She groaned when she heard him turn on the shower. There was no question that Mark was a hunk. Knowing he was less than ten feet from her made her knees tremble. *What would Roxanne do?* The answer to that was easy. What was *Mary* going to do? *"Nothing!"* her friend's voice ridiculed from the darkness.

The next sound Mary heard was Mark shaking out his sleeping bag. And fluffing his pillow. He made a big deal out of fluffing his pillow. There was something else. She was sure she heard another laugh when she scooted to the bathroom to get ready for bed. He was laughing at her. She was sure of it. And why shouldn't he?

Kate was due in soon, so any thought of giving in and crawling into Mark's sleeping bag with him was pointless, even if she could find the nerve which, of course, she couldn't. By the time Kate's friends dropped her off in her driveway, Mark was already fast asleep. *How could he do that? How could he make a pass at her and then just go to sleep?* Mary was in her bedroom, wide awake, curled up into a tight, fetal position, with her pillow over her head so she couldn't hear the soft gentle breathing of a man who was totally at ease on her living room floor. For now.

The next morning, Mary heated up the coffee that Mark had left in the pot and swore that it, too, was laughing at her. The living room was neat as a pin, and only a slightly wrinkled pillow rested in the easy chair. She resisted the urge to stop and fluff it.

4
Lousy at vacations

It was just as well Mary had never been serious about having company with her on her vacation. If Mark saw her with another man the whole family might know before she unpacked her pineapple.

She dashed into Roxanne's office and groaned into her coffee cup as she sat down. She screamed when she took a big gulp.

"Hot, huh?"

Too busy trying to keep the coffee from running out of her mouth and onto her silk blouse to answer, Mary could only shake her head as she ran to the trash basket so that the extra drips wouldn't get on Roxanne's carpet.

"So why are you in my office swilling coffee and spitting in my trash basket? What's up?"

"Oh, my gosh! Mark made a pass at me last night," Mary shrieked.

"Isn't that incest? Or at least ex-incest?"

"I don't think there's any such thing when it's the married side of the family. He says he'll see me in Hawaii."

"Now you've exchanged your fantasy beach buddy for a built-in spy. You're lousy at vacations, you know that? What does this guy look like, anyway?"

"Like my ex, only a year younger. Taller, thinner, with blue eyes, dark hair, and a tan."

"He sounds like a real loser," Roxanne kidded, "isn't he the park ranger?"

Still trying to recover from the hot coffee, Mary just nodded.

"That explains the tan. Around here, a tan usually means he's unemployed and has time to go to cancer-in-the-box everyday."

"Oh, he works, but in Montana."

"Wonderful! Lot's of job opportunities in your line of work there. What are you thinking?"

"I'm not thinking. I mean I didn't do anything," Mary said as she started on the second cup of coffee.

"Hello, Ladies, coffee break!" It was Ray, the layout guy, carrying a whole paper tray of expensive hot lattes.

"Ray, did you win the lottery?" Roxanne asked.

"No, I'm trying the win the heart of the new espresso boy at Wizard's. I keep buying coffee and my office is full of this stuff. Help me out, will you?"

Mary looked at the coffee warily. "Is any of this stuff decaf?"

"You want decaf? I'll be right back," their love struck friend said as he turned for the door.

"Sit down, cutie," Roxanne said. "Help me pound some sense into our friend here before she makes a big mistake and ends up writing stories for bear and moose in Montana."

"What? You're leaving us?"

"No! I'm just having an ex-family problem. My ex-brother-in-law is going to be in Hawaii at the same time I am."

"And that's a problem because?" Ray looked at Mary, and waited for more information.

"He's a hunk," Mary said.

"Oh, now I'm starting to catch up. Has anyone ever married her ex-brother-in-law and lived happily ever after?"

"No!" shouted Roxanne.

"Why not?" Ray asked.

"Geez, Louise! I've got two babes-in-woods here. Hasn't anyone but me ever been out in the real world?" Roxanne asked.

"Happy Thanksgiving! Imagine the table: your ex-mother-in-law, ex-dad-in-law, ex-husband, ex-husband's current squeeze, you, and your ex-brother-in-law who is now the designated boy-friend," she held one hand up, and rotated the other as if she were filming a documentary.

"E-uuuw!" Ray and Mary groaned.

"Instant replay at Christmas, Easter and the whole rest of your life. And who was it who told me last year that the best thing about being rid of the ex was being rid of the ex's fam? Do you really want to jump back into all of that stress?"

"I think I'm going to be sick," Mary said, as she reached for another cup of coffee. "This one's for the road, Ray, thanks. And good luck with the new hottie at Wizard's."

"Where you off to?" Roxanne asked.

"I have to deliver a contract to the ad department and have them cut me a check."

"You sold that ad? I didn't know you had a gun."

"Didn't need one. You won't believe what kind of an ad that old lady bought."

"Tell us!" they both cried.

"The woman is recycling pet sperm," she said as she quickly left the room. The loud gasp from her two friends made her giggle. She'd fill them in later.

Mary dropped the ad off but didn't ask for another. The package she'd sold was much larger than she'd expected, and she was running out of time. After she got back from the advertising de-partment, she picked up the extension and told Roxanne, "The next thing I want to do is go up to the roof and drop some poor helpless turtles onto the parking lot below."

"Must be the caffeine, it's making you mean."

"Ya think drinking an equal amount of decaf Wizard's would neutralize out the meanness?"

"Not likely. Besides, it's almost lunchtime."

"Yeah, a sandwich is probably in order. I fled out of the house without my morning cereal right after I got a whiff of after-shave lotion while I was brushing my teeth." She didn't mention that she gave herself points for not picking up Mark's towel and sniffing it before she left.

"Tell me, oh young and inexperienced, is there anything you *don't* run from?"

Mary cut her off, "Are we lunching, Old Wise One, or are you rushing off to meet some guy on a Harley?"

"We're lunching, Young Wussy One. I'll drive, since you're still wired on Nigerian caffeine. Wait for me while I go to the little girl's room. I don't like restaurant bathrooms."

Mary was waiting outside in the hallway when Roxanne came out of the bathroom.

"Where to? Ivar's for fish and chips? Dick's for burgers and fries? Lee's for stir fry?" Roxanne asked.

Mary tried to sort out the choices as she put on her seatbelt in Roxanne's car. "It's too cold to sit outside at Ivar's and their wind shelter will be swamped. Lee's might cut my Visa in half."

"Dick's it is, then."

"Oh, Roxanne, I'm feeling real queasy. I've got to dilute that coffee with some food, fast."

"If I'd have known that, we'd have taken *your* car; don't throw up!" To distract Mary from her jittery stomach, she asked, "What was that about recycling sperm?"

"Not now, Roxanne, not now," Mary pleaded as she rolled her forehead against the cool, car window.

Dick's, a Seattle favorite for hamburgers largely because it still made its hamburgers from real meat and its fries from real potatoes, was crowded as usual. Mary grabbed the first empty booth while Roxanne stood in line.

"So," Roxanne asked when she brought the food, "what are you going to do about your Montana hunk?"

"Well, maybe he's a good thing. He might be nice to go out to dinner with and good company at the beach, if he has time. It's unlikely I'll meet anyone else there."

"Besides, you don't do well with men you *know*. A *stranger* could turn out to be downright dangerous. Geez, Louise, with your luck, he'd turn out to be some nut who was in Hawaii to track space aliens. And what about this Mark guy? Aren't you worried that he will tell all to his family before you get unpacked?"

"Well, at this point, I have more on him than he has on me. I could threaten to tell his mom he's hitting on his poor, innocent, little ex-sis-in-law." Mary chewed a french fry and added, "To be honest, I don't think he'd say anything to the family if he saw me with Elvis in Hawaii."

"Well, here's to *Blue Hawaii*," Roxanne said raising her paper cup. "If Elvis really were there, I'd go with you."

"Some people say they've seen him on the beach. Why don't you come?" Mary asked with sudden enthusiasm. "It would be fun with you there!"

"I would if I could, but I'm all out of vacation time," Roxanne downed the last of her shake. "Besides, this is your vision quest, not mine."

"Are you supposed to be drinking strawberry shakes on your diet?"

"Stop changing the subject. Where's Mark staying?"

"He says the whole group is tenting it on one of the state park beaches."

"They have state parks in Hawaii?"

"Would you believe they even have them in the Virgin Islands?"

"Now, who wouldn't love that?" Roxanne asked sarcastically, "No restaurants, no chocolates on the pillow, no locks on the door, no air conditioning, no masseuse. Plenty of bugs and who knows what else? What's not to love?" Roxanne quickly checked an incoming message on her phone, and decided it could wait until she got back to the office. "So, do you want a ride out to the airport on Thursday morning?"

"That would be great. I could buy you breakfast," Mary offered.

"Who wants to eat at four in the morning? I plan to slow down the car, roll you and your bags out onto the pavement in front of the sidewalk baggage-check counter, and floor it until I get back to my own bed."

"And what about work?"

"Oh, I'll saunter in about nine, then I'll work through lunch. With you gone, the only one to lunch with is Ray, and he never leaves Wizard's lately."

"Poor man. Think he has a chance with this barista guy?"

"I don't know. He's starting to age. I wish he'd pick one and settle down. It's no time to be hopping around. This guy is a real looker, and Ray isn't the only guy circling his espresso machine. Who knows how much hopping this guy's already done?" Roxanne lowered her voice and confided, "And, Mary. There's something else. He treats Ray like dirt. I don't like him."

"That's not good; Ray's such a nice guy. But he's not the only person in our group who needs to pick one and settle down, you know."

"I know, I know. But I'm being more careful, I really am. And I'm thinking of getting married."

"To *whom*?"

"I don't know, but he'll have a yacht."

"Well, as long as we have our priorities in order."

"Oh, right. What I'm *really* looking for is an overweight loser with no prospects and a house full of rottweilers. Maybe he'll have a beer can collection, and live in his mother's basement."

"I take it all back. Follow that yacht."

After shaking all of the food wrappers to make sure a french fry or onion ring hadn't escaped notice, the two headed back to the office. Roxanne was on her way to mail out media packs to prospective advertisers, and Mary was off to research her next story so she'd be ready to put it together when she returned.

"What is this story you're on?"

"There's some new research I'm looking at on what turtles and frogs do in the winter."

"What do they do?"

"What's interesting is what they *don't* do. They don't always bury themselves in mud like we used to think they did. Scientists put tiny transmitters on them so they could track their movements. They've discovered those little guys move all over the place underwater around here as long as it's not too cold. They'd make a good cover, but our editor isn't into frogs and turtles. I'm hoping like heck he doesn't fish."

"Why is that?"

"Because then he might think that one of my other stories, giant Palouse Worms, would be a good cover."

"What do you mean giant?"

"They can be over three feet long."

"Go with the turtles and frogs if the other ideas don't pan out," Roxanne pleaded. "Here's another story idea: do you know why the Skagit Valley floods every spring?"

"No, why?"

"Because Hillary Clinton took all the dykes to Washington, DC."

"That's not funny, who told you that?"

"Ray."

"*Now*, it's funny!"

That night, Mary went home and cut the tags off the new clothes she'd bought for a trip she'd never taken because of her divorce. Earlier that night, she and Kate had gone out to dinner before Mary dropped her off at her grandmother's. The next morning, she'd be on her way. There was a part of Mary that kept shouting, *This is the stupidest thing you've ever done. If a vacation is giving you so much stress, maybe you shouldn't go.* The other part of her growled, s*hut-up and pack!*

The next morning, Roxanne showed up right on time. She handed Mary a commuter cup when she got into the car. "E-uuuw...what is this stuff?" Mary asked after a big sip.

"It's a protein shake with flax seed."

"Augh! Did someone steal your coffeepot?"

"I have one every morning. They're good for your cholesterol."

"I never worry about my cholesterol until I've had at least three cups of coffee."

True to her word, Roxanne rolled Mary out onto the pavement in front of the baggage checker and was gone before Mary got her ticket out of her purse. Suffering from a humongous anxiety attack, Mary would have gladly changed places with the little man tagging luggage and sent him in her place. She wondered how he'd get along with Mark.

On the plane, she buckled her belt and fought her urge to flee. The flight steward came along with coffee and magazines just as Mary was beginning to lose the battle. Until she dozed off, she sipped her coffee and flipped through magazines and played best case/worse case scenarios in her mind about how her vacation would turn out:

Good vacation/bad vacation.

Good Mark/horrible, repulsive Mark.

Casual date/no date at all.

Lost at sea/eaten by huge shark.

This last possibility appealed to her most. It could be a win-win situation. She'd get out of her vacation and the shark would get lunch.

The shark possibility hadn't occurred to Roxanne, who predicted she'd spend the whole vacation in her room, hiding under her bed. But, if she lacked a cooperative shark, a large part of Mary felt that the best possible outcome might be if Mark showed up at her hotel with a Hawaiian dancer in a grass skirt tucked under his arm. Then, all decisions would be made for her and she could relax. Seeing Mark stirred feelings in her she wasn't ready for. It wasn't just that she was lonely. There was something very sweet and honest about the man. A voice deep inside was telling her this guy wasn't looking for a casual affair. He was one of those forever and ever guys. But, was she ready to be a forever and ever girl?

5
Bears in the Hibiscus

On the way from the airport in Honolulu to the hotel, Mary felt like her eyes were dilated; the sun was so bright. Even so, she couldn't keep from following each palm tree from its base all the way to the top where the greenery was, just to make sure each tree was as advertised on the travel brochure: picture perfect. By the time her cab reached the hotel, she'd assured herself that all of the trees were intact, and all of those lovely flowers along the road were indeed real. Not a plastic bud in the bunch. While she admired the banyan trees, her cabby pointed out the sharks swimming in the waves with the surfers. The waves were backlit by sunlight that highlighted the sharks just under the surface of the water. He laughed that the surfers didn't know they were literally surfing with sharks. *What? They couldn't see a fish that big? Or did they think they were dolphins?*

At the hotel, the wall-to-wall mirror behind the check-in counter gave her a start. Next to all of the "locals," Mary looked ghost-like. The cashier didn't seem to notice her paleness when he handed her a key and a note from Mark, sealed in an envelope with the hotel's logo on it. In it, he said he was having a grand time and was thinking of applying for a grant to study trout in Hawaii for a couple of years. Then, he cautioned her to look out—there could be bears hiding in the hibiscus. He closed by saying he'd try to see her before he left. Just as Mary was finishing the note, the cashier handed her a paper bag full of tropical fruit. It had to be from Mark. He'd always been a grocery shopper. "Did all this fruit come with the note?" Mary asked the cashier.

"Yes Ma'am," the young boy grinned. "Mark said he'd gotten carried away at the local market. He had the entire sack laid out all over the counter, asking me what each piece was."

"That sounds like Mark. He's always been curious about foods." She wasn't surprised that the cashier knew his name. Mark was on a first-name basis with everyone he ever met. He was such a great guy. If only his last name wasn't Bergstrom.

From her room she could see the beach two blocks away. It looked wonderful, but she was tired, and couldn't work up the enthusiasm to leave the building. She decided to hit the hotel pool and then spend the leftover time before dinner on her lanai, sipping something cold while she worked on her journal of ways she could improve her life. She was relieved to get voicemail at her mother-in-law's, so she didn't have to speak to Elizabeth, Kate's grandmother. *What would she say if the woman asked her if she'd heard from Mark?* She left a quick message for Kate that said she'd arrived safely before she jumped into her swimsuit.

Not bad, she thought as she surveyed her slim body in her new, one-piece suit. Since her divorce, she'd dropped about thirty pounds. From what she'd heard, that was about the average amount of weight loss for a newly divorced woman re-entering the workplace. Unfortunately, she'd also been told that weight lost during the trauma of becoming single again always came back when the body adjusted to being alone and working a forty hour week.

The suit she'd picked out at the local department store before she left was not the type of clothing she usually wore, but that was the point in buying it. The black, slinky number with no built-in bra and fluorescent pink orchids all over the front felt right at home here. They'd had a similar suit in a bikini, but Mary wasn't quite ready to go *that* native. Besides, to Mary, the one-piece suit with a modest neckline sent a message: *I'm here to have a good time, and I'm approachable, but I am not loose.*

Mary had brought a *pareo* to tie around her waist, but opted for a long loose cover-up. It was a long way to the pool, and she'd have to take the elevator to the first floor. Besides, she might decide to take a short walk after her swim, and she wasn't sure what the sidewalk etiquette was in Honolulu.

When she got to the lobby, she struck up a short conversation with three sisters who'd made the trip to the islands from North Dakota. This was their third visit, and when Mary asked about good places to eat, they told her the outside cafeteria down the street was the best and cheapest fare around. Mary gratefully accepted their invitation to meet them underneath the big scallop shell lamp in the lobby around six for dinner. What a relief, having her meals alone had been one of the things she'd dreaded most.

At the pool, Mary was delighted to see lava rock with orchids in all colors growing out between the rocks in the landscaping. She slipped off her sandals and jumped into the water with such force that she knocked the scrunchie right out of her hair. She swam around for a few minutes looking for it, but it was the same color as the water, and there was no hope of finding it without her glasses. She looked high and low, unable to decide whether it would float or sink, but she finally gave up and forgot about it. When she made it to the other side of the pool, she dove deep and felt the cool water rush past her body like pulling a silk nightie over her head. The pool was deserted, so she wasn't concerned when the weight of the water pulled the neckline of her swimsuit much lower than it was designed to be worn. Lost in her own thoughts, she was startled to see men laughing and pointing from behind a glass wall near the bottom of the pool. They all seemed to be pointing in a certain direction. Mary looked and could barely make out the shape of her scrunchie floating in the middle of the pool, about halfway down. She looked at her body to see if the deep flush she felt showed. She was shocked to discover that one of her breasts was almost completely uncovered. Feeling exposed and stupid, she finally caught onto why she was lucky enough to have the whole pool to herself. No one else would agree to be a free floor show for the lounge lizards who, thanks to an architect's clever design, had a front row seat to what went on underwater in the pool. Later, she would be grateful she hadn't been pussy-footing around under the water with some guy, but for now, things were embarrassing enough.

Trying to act nonchalant, Mary stretched out in a lounge chair, but couldn't get her legs to stop shaking. She couldn't remember when she'd ever been so embarrassed. She put her sunglasses on and thought she might wear them for the rest of her trip. *If I had read the literature in my room that the hotel provided, I would have known about the lech-zone at the bottom of the pool,* she scolded herself. She wondered if they could see her lounging; she hoped not, but she was pretty sure she was still on full display. She was uneasy, but forced herself to stay for five minutes more before she ran out of the pool area. She bolted for the elevator just as the doors were closing; safely in, she looked out and saw the second one opening. One of the guys in the bar was headed through the lobby toward the pool. That was close. She shuddered at the thought of some boozer pulling a lounge chair close to hers and breathing his alcoholic breath in her face while he ogled her body.

The lanai off her room felt like heaven. Shady, scenic, and safe. As an added bonus, from eleven floors up, she had a panoramic view of the water. It should be a dynamite place to watch sunsets.

Mary settled on the chaise in her own little domain with relish and relief. Before she opened her journal, she was joined by a white dove that flew onto the lanai. The bird eyed its new visitor cautiously, but soon, the little creature became used to her and started cooing. As it nestled behind a huge potted plant in the corner of the lanai, it became clear that, to the bird, Mary was the intruder. *Why doesn't it roost in the plant? Maybe there were bears in the bush.* Mary playfully shook the bush's branches. *Nope, but then, it might not be a hibiscus.*

She allowed herself to doze and just be. This was, after all, what she'd come for. To just be, with no demands from lover, boss, or family. Even though she had her eyes shut, she was aware of the soft breeze blowing the white sheer curtains floating over the sliding glass door. There was something sensuous about their movement and not just because they were on a tropical island. Mary knew she'd have to get some billowy sheers for her bedroom at home.

In her relaxed mental state, her mind went back to her fantasy of a date on a yacht in the middle of Puget Sound. It was a comforting dream, and Mary saw no reason to change the boat's location to Hawaii. After all, it was just a fantasy, location wasn't important. Who was this man, anyway? He wasn't like anyone Mary was conscious of, but seemed to be a combination of several men she had dreamed about for years.

Thin, preppy, intellectual. The witty observer of political events. The successful businessman who can afford to have a cabin cruiser and not worry about the payments. The romantic. The creative craftsman who makes garden sculptures from recycled copper with his own hands.

All in one man.

But what would Mary be? A writer? An artist? A successful sales executive? She realized that making money would never, in reality, be in her cards, but in a fantasy she could be anything. She could run against the local powerful politician, and win. She could travel to China regularly to check on factory orders. She could be a chef of great Northwest Cuisine. This last one, Mary knew, was the greatest stretch. She'd be lucky if she ever learned to make a great sandwich. Even before her divorce, Mary was a plain cook, specializing in one-pot dinners that were timesavers and always left plenty of chicken and beef for another meal the next day. Surrounded by gardeners, a lot of her meals were planned around the surplus fresh fruits and vegetables her neighbors left on her back deck in huge stainless steel bowls. Mary used everything her neighbors shared with her, so her meals were delicious, but far from gourmet. So, she could never even fantasize about being a chef, but she could be a winemaker. *Yeah, that's what she was. She pictured herself with a little vineyard and neat bottles of her wines lined up on a rustic shelf. Her little tasting room nestles by the side of the road that followed the curves of Hood Canal. Her grapes are very special because the vines had been carried over the Oregon Trail in a covered wagon. Her gorgeous man in this fantasy is on a museum board, and calls to ask if he can have a tour of the vineyards. When their eyes meet, it is pure electricity.* Sort of. Hard as Mary tried, she kept seeing Mark's face where the Renaissance man's should be. She closed her eyes and looked closely at this intruder. Tall, dark, and good-looking, with a humorous expression, he was no Renaissance man, it was true. But he did have the possibility of a good roll in the hay.

Or sack.

Or sand.

Or *whatever*.

She looked down on the street and saw that people were dressed up in their muumuus and strolling towards the local restaurants. She was hungry, too. She had just enough time to shower and pull back her hair before she met her new friends in the lobby. Mary laid a long bone-colored linen shift on the bed. It was the closest thing to a muumuu she had. Maybe, if she got a muumuu while she was there, she could wear it several times to dinners. And big earrings. She was craving big earrings. She wasn't normally the big earring type; there must be something in the Hawaiian air. She resisted a yearning to tuck a gardenia from the hotel's garden in her hair. She'd already made a big enough fool of herself at the pool.

After she'd washed off her first day's pool water and looked at her bland image in the mirror, she suddenly remembered a shell necklace strung on a turquoise-colored cord Roxanne had picked up for her at a garage sale several months ago. Perfect! Maybe she could find some shell earrings to go with it in one of the local shops.

Mary saw her dinner companions the minute she got to the lobby. They were busily discussing how they could make a shell lamp just like the one hanging above them with a few shells and their trusty glue gun when they got home. *They probably could. Maybe she'd try it herself. She'd hang it between her Georgia O'Keefe print and the poster of a man tossing a big salmon in Pike's Place Market. Well, maybe not.* Decorating was another thing Mary wasn't known for, but even she recognized that mixing O'Keefe, salmon photos, and seashells would not get her a show on that television decorating channel.

The women were all wearing colorful muumuus they'd purchased the minute they'd gotten off the plane. They'd show her where, they promised. Jean, the youngest, had found a dress with a built-in bra. The other women just went braless, which wasn't even noticeable because of the loose fabric. Mary was tempted to do the same. It was hot and the humidity made her bra feel like it was made from the fibers of a coconut shell.

On the way to the ladies' favorite outdoor cafeteria, they passed several little trinket stands, and Mary found a pair of huge mother of pearl earrings with turquoise beads just like the ones she'd envisioned. Marge insisted they all stop so Mary could put them on right there on the street. Self-conscious at first, she soon realized no one else noticed. She could have changed her blouse and not caused a stir. So much for sidewalk etiquette.

As if to reiterate this observation, a middle-aged, plus-sized woman in a string bikini, flip-flops, and a big straw hat passed the group headed for the main drag in town. Mary hoped the woman wasn't headed for the pool at her hotel.

The outdoor cafeteria was everything her new friends had said it was: good and cheap. Mary loaded up on vegetables and a fish that was new to her: mahi mahi. Marge said it was really dolphin, but the other women said that wasn't true. It was a dolphinfish, that was a type of dolphin, but it wasn't a mammal. Mary didn't know who to believe. Just the idea of it possibly being dolphin would keep her from ordering it again. At home, their pantry had been stripped of any tuna that may have caused the death of a dolphin. The confusion over what the fish was—or wasn't—was a shame, because it was really delicious.

The outside eating area was dotted with palm trees and flowering bushes that Mary hadn't identified, but Marge, a gardener, identified the vines as bougainvillea, and the bushes as hibiscus. Mary checked behind the bushes, but they were bearless. All of the women had a good laugh when Mary explained why she was shaking the bushes. A soft breeze was kicking up, and the island's smells mixed together and made a heady perfume that was thick enough to land on Mary's skin. Perhaps she'd wasted her money on that gardenia perfume she'd bought when she'd stopped to buy her earrings.

During dinner, Mary learned a lot about her new companions. The three of them lived in Grand Forks, North Dakota, and Lucille and Marge were widows. Jean was married, but her husband was a woodworker, and preferred to spend his free time in his woodshop. None of the women were complaining. In George, they had a willing carpenter, painter and plumber, all in one handy, friendly package. To hear the women talk, their homes were all filled with beautiful cabinets made by Jean's home-loving husband. The sisters had started taking trips to tropical locations when Lucille lost her husband. They'd tried the Bahamas and Mexico, but had settled on Hawaii as their favorite because it was friendlier, and the food was better in the middle-of-the-road price range.

Jean was convinced, and they all agreed, that any restaurant could serve a decent meal if they plopped seventy-five bucks on the table. The women weren't budgeting, but they had a respect for money that developed over the years. Sitting in front of a beautiful plate with fresh fish, vegetables and iced tea, all for twenty dollars, Mary couldn't disagree.

After dinner, they took a walk past the nightclubs and restaurants. Jean laughed when she saw the sign on one bragging that customers could cook their own steak. "I do that at home... why on earth would I want to stand over a hot greasy grill when I'm all dressed up?" she asked. When they peeked in, they discovered it was mostly full of young people in their twenties and thirties.

"Maybe if they're lucky," Marge mused, "they can wash their own dishes."

"And put out the cat!" laughed Jean.

They wanted to walk on the beach, but they'd all worn their good sandals, and women in their age group with their medical problems didn't walk on the beach barefooted and chance a cut foot. It was okay with Mary, she'd had a long day and was ready to go back to her room, get ready for bed, and watch the breeze blow her sheers. On the way back to the hotel, she told the women about her experience in the pool, and the women hooted when Lucille threatened to put on her one-piece, size 2X, with the pleated skirt, and give the lounge boys a thrill.

When Mary got to her room she found a phone message from Mark that said he wanted to take her to a luau with his park ranger friends the next night. He'd pick her up in a rented car at eight o'clock.

Mary was a little uneasy with the invitation, but it sounded like fun. She knew she'd never last until eight or after on an empty stomach. She'd better grab a quick bite when she got in from the beach.

She also had a message from Kate that said she had joined a motorcycle gang and planned to cover herself in tattoos. Reading between the lines, Mary surmised that the visit with her grandmother wasn't going so badly, after all.

6
Can you say lobster?

Mary was one of the first ones on the beach the next day. She carried her towel and a tote bag full of necessities she would need to spend the day, along with her breakfast of a cup of coffee and a macadamia muffin she'd picked up. The shade between the hotels was cool on her way to the water, but it started to heat up impressively when she hit the sand. She heard someone say that the temperature was expected to reach eighty-eight; Mary couldn't wait. It had been a long, dreary, winter in the Northwest, and it wasn't just the weather that she'd found lacking. Anxious to wash away a winter full of regrets, financial struggle, and overwork, she pulled on her snorkel and hit the water. She was aware she was in a tropical paradise, but she was unprepared for the abundance of color she saw in water not over eight feet deep. Fish of all shapes and colors seemed to be waiting in that very spot just for her. For the first time, she wished for a companion to share it with. Lacking a partner, she imagined herself as one of the finned creatures, swimming in clear, blue water that was more like the water in an aquarium tank than the ocean. With complete abandon, she followed one colorful school after another. Before she realized it, she'd snorkeled way beyond her physical limits. That was when she remembered the taxi driver who had pointed out the sharks at the surfers' park. The water she was in was easily as deep. Terrified to the point of almost being immobilized, she turned around and cautiously made her way back to shallower waters. She had seen a movie once where a swimmer panicked and kicked so hard he attracted killer sharks.

All the while she kicked, she was aware of her heart racing, and she couldn't stop herself from twisting her neck back and forth to look for big fish with teeth to match. *What was that old adage? Never swim alone? But what good would a swimming partner do her in this situation, besides give the shark a choice?*

Mary didn't remember seeing one tropical fish once she'd gotten into deep water. She wondered why she didn't turn around and go back when the little schools of fish did. When she neared the beach, she began to notice them again. She wondered if fish were like the birds in her backyard at home. Some of them only ate seeds on the ground. Other birds only fed several feet off the ground. Still others fed at higher levels. It made sense for fish, too, only in reverse. The deeper the water, the bigger the fish? This was one of those questions she'd rather research at the library. After a rest, on her next venture into aquatic paradise, she planned to snorkel in a direction horizontal to the shore where the smaller fish were. The surfers could have the sharks.

But first, she needed to rest. She breathed slowly and waited for her heart to settle down. A few women had moved in nearby, and Mary looked for the three Grand-Forkers, but they were nowhere to be seen. They'd probably hit the shops first. Anyway, they'd all mentioned their concerns about getting too much sun, and Jean, with her red hair, was sure she'd be the first to turn into toast.

Mary figured she'd better cut her first day short to avoid looking like a total fool at the luau that night. Besides, she was feeling uneasy about her wardrobe. The natural linen dress she'd brought from home looked way too plain, too beige, and most of all, too stodgy to be worn here. Certainly, it would be out of place at a luau. The long linen sheath was not only bland, but it didn't have a kick pleat. Would she be able to walk in it on the beach? It wasn't difficult to convince herself that she should follow the Grand-Forkers' advice to swing by one of the local shops and buy a muumuu. She wanted one anyway, for a souvenir of her trip; she might as well put it to good use.

As much as she told herself she'd stayed in the sun too long, she just couldn't seem to pack up and go. It was almost three before Mary left the beach, and that was only because she was hungry. She was on her way back to her room with a take-out salad when she ran into her new friends, laden down with bags from the local shops. They were excited to see Mary because one of the shops was having a sale, and they'd talked the manager into putting some muumuus aside for her to try on. When they found out she was going to a luau, they became even more enthused.

"Look," Lucille said, "he'll hold them until six. Why don't you eat your salad, get ready for the luau and run over while you're waiting for your guy? We could even go with you! What fun!"

Mary laughed and agreed to meet the women underneath the giant sea shell chandelier in an hour. As she went back to her room, she happily admitted to herself that she was grateful for the friendly company. Her house at home was usually a swinging door for her and Kate's friends, and she was feeling a little lonesome in this paradise of waving palm trees and bougainvillea vines. However, she wasn't lonesome enough to practice her come hither look on the sexy men on the beach wearing minimal swim trunks and little else. They seemed to be everywhere she looked today, nonchalantly spreading sun tan lotion on their overly exposed bodies. For years, she'd heard jokes about men's revealing swimwear on the beaches, but she wasn't prepared for the reality of a man—thin or fat—in a Speedo. *What were they thinking?* She couldn't bring herself to look at their faces for fear she'd recognize some of them from the lounge at the bottom of the pool.

She planned to spend the hours before Mark picked her up sitting on her lanai and reviewing her life's options, but that probably could wait a day or so. Besides, no matter how many times she went over her finances and future prospects, the numbers were always bleak. Things would be tight until she got Kate though high school and four years of college. Her daughter had a trust fund to help her with her higher education, but Mary didn't know if it would be enough. Largely, it depended upon what school Kate picked and whether or not she got a scholarship. So what good was worrying? She may as well shop. At sale prices, maybe she could even pick up a little something for Kate. She'd been wondering what she could take her.

Mary finished her salad, and headed for the shower. She noticed her skin was rapidly changing colors. *Can you say lobster?* she said as she surveyed her body in the bathroom mirror. *Good thing you exercised some restraint on your first day, kiddo. One more hour and your skin would be ready for a little teriyaki sauce.* It was too hot to turn on a hair dryer, so Mary pulled her hair back and put another scrunchie on it. She had a fleeting thought that the colorful accessory that she had a whole sack of was now considered dorky, but she doubted if the company she would be keeping at the luau would be up on the latest fashions. Her ex-mother-in-law would frown, Mary knew. But then, Elizabeth was the kind of woman who could go to the beach with a rhinestone brooch pinned to her swimsuit, and no one would raise an eyebrow.

When Mary reached the lobby, the other women were already there. Each woman had a paper cup with crushed ice and an unspecified liquid. Mary was sure she got a whiff of rum, but Marge assured her it was harmless, just a combination of all of the little liquor bottles they'd found at the bottoms of their purses and some fresh pineapple juice. Lucille giggled and pulled one out of her huge silver metallic tote bag for Mary.

It was really a shame they didn't have a recipe for their concoction. It was darn good. They walked down the sidewalk, their tote bags and hips bumping into each other as they sipped their cocktails. When they went into the shop, the women were greeted like they were relatives of the first cruise ship off the shores of Oahu. The girls made themselves comfortable while Mary headed for the dressing room. Out of the corner of her eye she saw Lucille pull out yet another cocktail from her purse and hand it to the store manager. When she hung the dresses on a hook in the dressing room, she was impressed with the choices of her friends, but it was obvious they were too expensive for her budget. She was wondering how she'd tell them after they'd gone to so much trouble when she looked down and saw the prices; they were all fifty percent off!

The long muumuu was really beautiful, but Mary was afraid it looked too dressy for a beach party with a bunch of inebriated park rangers. Nonetheless, she slipped it on and went out to show her fashion scouts. "Oh!" Marge exclaimed; you look like a princess. Try on the others!" After all of the outfits had been tried on and modeled for her friends, Mary was trying to decide between the short muumuu in the turquoise and white print with an elastic front neckline, or a muumuu pantsuit in red and white. She decided on the short number with the elastic because the pantsuit looked too dressy for the company she'd be keeping. Then she asked to see something in a size four for Kate. The shopkeeper came back with the perfect short Hawaiian print muumuu. She laughed and told her friends it must be time to go; her charge card was full and her cup was empty. High on bargains, the women laughed all the way back to the hotel. On the way, they told Mary they'd each bought over four hundred dollars worth of dresses at the store for themselves and friends back home. No wonder they were on a drinking basis with the manager. Mary wouldn't have been surprised if *he* provided the drinks.

When she went back to her room to wait for Mark, there was a message for her from Kate that said she left the motorcycle gang, and had fallen in love with a circus clown; she was going on the circuit with him. Of course, they'd be sleeping with the elephants.

7

Pineapple park rangers

Mary looked at the clock in her room; it was only seven. She had a long time to wait until Mark picked her up at eight. She wished she had another one of the girls' special drinks, but she settled instead for a cold cola from the machine at the end of the hall and a bucket of ice. The ice was for her arms and back. It was beginning to feel as if the lobster-colored burn on her back was growing a tail and claws. Mary decided the real traditional Hawaiian cocktail, for tourists at least, was a cola and two aspirin. The pineapple filled with frothy, alcoholic liquid she saw on Hawaiian television shows was strictly for the islanders, who were pain-free due to an abundance of skin pigment and brain cells.

The ice felt so good on her shoulders, she stripped down to her panties and rubbed it everywhere she could reach. A sudden pain in her sandals announced the arrival of severe, painful sunburn on the tops of her feet. She should cancel her date with Mark, but she didn't have a phone number. *He'll probably take one look at me and leave me at the hotel anyway,* she thought.

She planned to sit on the lanai, but the bed won out. Mary crawled in and prayed for a merciful park ranger to find another date for tonight. Maybe one of those bears he'd been talking about on the island. Anyone or *anything* but her.

The aspirin began to take effect and Mary became oblivious to the sheets tearing at her skin and fell asleep with her arms and legs stretched out so that no part of her body was touching that didn't absolutely have to. *Levitation. Levitation would be good. Oh, if only it were possible.* Mary fell asleep—or maybe passed out—before she took off her sunglasses. Laughter in the halls and the rattling elevator door woke her up a few minutes before Mark was supposed to pick her up. Her heart thumped. *Was that Mark?* Had she locked her door? It wasn't, and she had. It wasn't like Mary to have embarrassing incidents, and she didn't like the new trend she was setting. But it was time to get up and dress. Her new outfit had soft elastic around the shoulders, and fit loosely. Even so, Mary could feel the fabric chewing on her skin. What would she have done if she'd had to wear her linen outfit? Mary imagined blood seeping through the natural linen at the shoulders. She hadn't just shopped when she'd purchased her new muumuu, she'd saved herself from a slow, Hawaiian death. Mary quickly pulled her hair back, changed the scrunchie in her hair to match her new outfit, and added her new shell earrings that matched her necklace. She had too much sunburn to even consider putting on make-up. All she had to do was pack her camera and an extra roll of film and she'd be ready. No, wait, she'd better take a swimsuit and towel. She had a moment's hesitation when she stuffed her slinky swimsuit into her tote bag. When she bought it, she'd never imagined that anyone she knew would see her in it. Her faced burned when she pictured Mark looking at the soft mounds of her unrestrained breasts filling out the top of her suit, but she resisted throwing in a tee-shirt to wear over it. *Oh, grow up!* She chided herself. *The man is as old as I am. He's seen breasts before. Most of them bigger than mine,* she thought with chagrin.

As it turned out, Mark never came up, he just buzzed her from the lobby. As Mary closed the door on her room, she glanced at the rumpled bedspread and assorted first aid supplies scattered around her bed. Obviously, she hadn't given any thought to Mark coming up to her room when he brought her home.

Mark greeted Mary like a favorite sister, and didn't mention her new outfit, for which Mary was grateful. She was a little uncomfortable with her ex-husband's brother, and didn't know quite how to act, until she glanced in the backseat and saw it was crammed with paper sacks filled with groceries. The Montana Park Ranger had been hitting the stores again. Mary laughed and let her head rest against the car seat. There was nothing to fear. Mark was Mark. Easy-going, personable, and the exact opposite of his brother.

"I see you threw your good sense and sunscreen to the winds. How long were you out today?"

"Don't know, cooked too many brain cells," Mary answered. "What did you do?"

"I went on a tour of the state parks on Oahu. They've got some great snorkeling and diving here. They say the visibility is one-hundred feet or more. I've just been snorkeling because I'm not a diver, but there's plenty to see without strapping on air tanks," Mark said enthusiastically. "It's too bad I don't have a degree in marine biology. Now that I've seen what's underwater here, I'm curious about what's under the surface in my own lake at the park. Probably just trout, but who knows? There could be something no one has ever seen down there. At the very least, there could be some freshwater shrimp. Some of our lakes have them. No one has ever looked around there. Anyway, I have to bring the girls back here someday. They would love it."

"So would Kate," agreed Mary. She wanted to tell him about her snorkeling experience, but she didn't have the energy; she'd tell him later. "How's it going with the other visiting rangers?" she asked instead.

"Great. We've even got some representatives from Alaska. They brought a whole box of frozen moose dogs to cook on the beach."

"Moose dogs?"

"Yeah. Huge hot dogs made from moose. They're delicious, I hear, and low fat. We'll try some tonight."

"Since when did you become worried about fat?"

"I'm not, just repeating the sales pitch I heard. Some guy from California is bringing cases of wine, and a guy from Washington is bringing a couple of kegs of micro beer."

"So, what's in the backseat?"

"Just some paper plates and cups. Oh, I also picked up some T-bones, potatoes, and a big coffeepot so we can make some coffee on the beach with the Wizard's that showed up in the camp kitchen. There are also Hawaiian dishes, casseroles from Mexico, and caribou sausages from Canada."

"That's a lot of food. Did they have room for clothes?"

"No, they're all naked as spiny lobsters, and about the same color. You'll fit right in. And I don't want *my* lobster getting in any car that's driven by one of my ranger buddies. If they need to run any errands, come and get me. I've taken to following them from beach to beach in my own car because they drive like complete idiots when they're sober. Who knows what they'll be like tonight?"

"Got ya...thanks for the heads up. Do they do this often?"

"Yeah. They move around. Christmas is going to be at my lodge. Some of these guys have never seen a Christmas tree and snow except in the movies, so I'm going to do the whole White Christmas thing. I'm looking forward to it. Linda is taking the kids back east to spend Christmas with her parents, so I imagine I'll be glad for the company."

"What's she been up to lately?"

"Oh, the three Ws, working, whining, and whoring..."

"Now, that's attractive."

"Sorry, but she keeps bringing strange men home in the middle of the night. The girls never know who they're going to find in the kitchen in the morning, usually standing in front of the coffeepot scratching their butt in their underwear."

"Oh, my dates do that all the time."

"Right. When I spent the night, I saw how comfortable you are with men when I was on your sundeck. Do you always panic and blow red wine out your nose when a man makes a pass at you?"

"Hey!" Mary laughed and tried to refocus the attention on Linda. "Where does she meet all these guys? Men hardly ever ask me out."

"They don't ask *her* out either. They ask her *in*…or they ask her to go on out-of-town business trips with them."

"All you men are alike and I don't believe a word of it. Besides, when did you move into the monastery?"

"When the local girls saw my empty checkbook. And, keep in mind, there aren't that many women in the mountains. My closest neighbor is a guy. Jackson Boss, ever heard of him?"

"His name sounds familiar."

"He owns that big outdoor recreation company, Nisqually Jack's."

"Oh? What's he like?"

"Real nice person. He's one of those guys that it's hard to see how he got so far, he's so laid back. We go fishing a lot. Sometimes, he puts floats on his plane so we can land right on the water."

"He flies his own plane? Is that safe?"

"The way he does it, it is. I'd fly with him anywhere. Sometimes, he flies me around for the forest service. Our budget is too low to have our own plane," he shook his head. "If Congress makes anymore cuts, I know some guys who are going to have to start a black market in fish and game just to make ends meet. Here we are," Mark said as he pulled into a parking lot, "let's take down the stuff in the backseat and I'll introduce you to everybody."

Mary followed Mark to a picnic area that had three tables piled with food and drink, and a huge campfire, but only about eight people were there, dancing to a raucous CD that seemed to be a local Hawaiian band. "Where is everybody?" asked Mark.

"Well, Kono took eight of the rangers who wanted to night dive out in his boat, then we've got some more doing a forced march on the beach, and some lovebirds here and there in the bushes," said Halo, a Hawaiian who had a smile bigger than the Milky Way.

"Okay," Mark stopped him, "I get the idea. Meet Mary. She's family, so treat her nice."

"*Aloha*, wine or beer?"

"Wine, please, red if you have it."

"We do. Short on the white, though. We started out with a big wash tub of it because we were going to bob for mangos, but some guy from Alaska tried to put out a fire with it. Saw it in the tub and assumed it was water."

"Was he hurt?" Mary asked.

"Naw...he just lost some of his eyebrows. He's out on the dive now." Halo handed her a big plastic cup of red wine. "*Okole Maluna*!"

When Mary looked at him quizzically, he explained, "Bottoms up!"

Before she had her first sip, Mary felt big arms around her and looked down to see a grass skirt being wrapped around her waist by her Hawaiian host. The grass rustled softly with his movements, and Mary thought it must have just been made, because it still smelled green. "There. Now nobody tell you from long-time native girl," the big ranger said playfully.

"Thank you, Halo," Mary said.

"*Kipa Mai*," Halo answered.

Mary gave it a few playful shakes and Halo fell to the ground, seemingly overcome by her wiles.

Mark reached over and poured a cup of beer on his face, and repeated, "I told you, this one's family; go find your own grass skirt."

"Hey, man," Halo teased, "she's *your* family, not *mine*," then he continued, "well, if I can't flirt with the mainlander, let's eat. Grab a plate, everybody. We're not going to wait for the divers. They won't be back until they run out of air."

Mary filled her plate with piles of the native fruits and a taste of the poi; she wasn't sure what it was or even if it was cooked, and didn't want to ask. *How could she not know? She'd heard about it for years.*

Mark wasn't nearly so shy. "Halo, what is this?" he asked.

"Oh, that?" Halo answered, "It's poi, I picked it up at the local deli just to make the table look Hawaiian. I never touch the stuff myself."

"What's in it?"

"Basically, it's just a root called taro that we dig up and pound into a paste. Sort of our version of mashed potatoes," he said unenthusiastically.

"You're quite a salesman," Mark said.

Halo laughed, "The last time we took mainlanders fishing, one of them threw it over the side of the boat. He thought it was bait."

"Okkaay, moving right along, papaya. That I can handle!" Mark said.

"I can vouch for the pork ribs. My mom makes them with a ginger teriyaki," Halo said.

Mary wished his mom had come with Halo, so she could have gotten the recipe. They were definitely the best. First, they tasted sweet, then spicy, then hot, until Mary had to consciously stop herself from sucking on the bones.

It was a beautiful evening with stars thicker than rhinestones on a Las Vegas tee-shirt. She was aware she was feeling a buzz from the wine Halo had given her. How many glasses had she had? Two, three? Someone had put on a country western CD, and she heard a mournful voice singing about his lost loves, each one of whom had left with one of his pickup trucks. It was obvious the singer missed the trucks more than he did the women. Mark took one look at Mary and took her plate and set it behind them on the table. "Let's take a walk, you're getting weepy-eyed on me." Mary took off the grass skirt because she'd never walked on a beach when she hadn't gotten too close to the water. "So what's the problem, you still moaning over my self-centered brother? Haven't you heard the only lady he can keep is a bug?"

"Yeah, so Kate says."

"He might be a dynamite businessman, Mary, but he's a loser after 5:00. But if you want him back, I'll help all I can," he said sadly.

"No, Mark, I don't want him back. I'm just tired of being alone."

"What am I? Chopped poi?!"

"No, you're great," Mary laughed, "I'm sorry. And, according to you, I'm family."

Mark drew her close and kissed her long and hard. "Welcome to Hawaii, little sister."

"Did anyone ever tell you you're a great kisser?"

"Yeah, and according to my ex-wife, I make love a lot better than my brother, too."

Startled, Mary looked up. "Don't ask, it's the booze talking," Mark whispered, "I shouldn't have said anything and you don't want to know."

He was right. "See Mark? This is what I worry about. Here we are, maybe beginning a new relationship, and we're dragging all of the baggage from our past relationships behind us. And to be honest, I have reservations about rejoining the whole family." Her brain was getting fuzzy, and she had to struggle to finish her thought. "I don't think I'll ever be able to measure up to your mother and dad's standard of success."

"You're wrong about mom. She wasn't always president of the Women's Republican Committee. She stayed home and raised Brian and me just like you're raising Kate. She has always thought you were the best. Dad can be difficult. But he's that way with most people. He's just not the warm and fuzzy type, not even with Brian and me," Mark admitted.

Mary wanted to believe Mark, and the booze helped her loosen her resolve. She wasn't even upset about Brian and Linda having an affair. Whatever their ex-spouses were doing, it was on their own time, and this was her time.

She lifted her lips to Mark's and leaned into his body, savoring his manliness and the moment. She'd been alone since her divorce, and her body was hungry for everything Mark had to offer. The closer she got, the more she realized that he did, indeed, *have* a lot to offer.

Mark pulled away to get a breath and was startled when Mary lost her balance. "Mary, you're drunk!"

She was embarrassed to tell him that part of her wobbliness was his fault, and not the booze. Maybe almost all of it. "No, no, I'm not."

"Yes, yes, you are. I don't want you to sober up tomorrow and think I took advantage of you. Let's rejoin the group. It looks like the divers are back."

Mary was angry; she pulled up her fist, fully intending to punch him in the stomach, but he caught it and brought it to his lips, then drew her body into his chest, and held her there until she stopped shaking. While he held her, he whispered in her ear, "We've both been alone too long, but not like this, Mary. Come on, let's go get your grass skirt. Nobody can be sad wearing one of those things."

Mary put on her best face, not wanting to share her feelings with a group of strangers, besides, Mark had to socialize with them the rest of the week. She didn't want to embarrass him in front of his new friends. As she waded through a pile of dive gear to get to the table, someone handed her a cold, icy fruit drink. Mary gulped it down; too late, she realized it was loaded with booze. Oh, well, what the hell? She reached for another, and handed one to Mark. After all, it wasn't *his* fault she'd over-imbibed, and it wasn't *his* fault she was his ex-sister-in-law, and it also wasn't *his* fault he had a rich, driven family. But it *was* his fault he had much higher morals than his brother. Mary usually admired that in a man, but not tonight. Tonight she was look-ing for a man who'd roll her in the sand and pull her dress up over her head. *Was that too much to ask? What the hell else was a Hawaiian beach for?*

The next morning she woke up alone in Mark's tent. She vaguely remembered him saying he was too drunk to drive, and that she could sleep in his tent, and he'd bunk with one of the guys. All through the night she'd heard laughter and song, and felt nothing but admiration for bodies that were conditioned to stay up all night partying. She didn't think she was ever like that. Even in college, she'd always been the first to call it a night. The next morning, she was always told that she'd missed all of the fun.

Mary looked down to see she'd taken her dress off last night, and it was neatly laid out next to her sleeping bag. She *did*, didn't she? Oh, she hoped she did. *Oh, please, I didn't let Mark undress me.* She tried to remember, but all that came to mind was that her head hurt. Mark popped his head into the tent and offered her breakfast, but she declined. "Just, please, Mark, take me back to the hotel and let me die in my own rented bed."

"Okay, but you'll miss the ride in the canoe and the spreading of the rancid poi over the rolling waves of Kaneohe Bay."

"Mark, I've never known you to be mean, much less downright cruel."

"Uh, you might want to put that dress back on before you make a dash for the car."

Mary looked down to see she was mostly uncovered from the waist up; she must still be drunk, or she would have noticed she was unclothed around a man. *Any* man, not to mention a hunk like Mark.

Mary threw her dress on and ran to the car and, finding it mercifully unlocked, climbed in and tried to melt into the seat covers. As soon as Mark turned onto the highway, she took a breath and said, "Mark, I'm so sorry, you know I'm not used to drinking, but that's no excuse. I don't know what happened."

"Not to worry. *I* know what happened. I asked Halo what was in that fruit drink. Turns out it was some kind of fermented tropical fruit mixture his mom made up once to seduce his dad, and it's become a household staple every since. After I left you in the tent, I barely made it back to the gang before I passed out myself. How's your head?"

"It hurts. Does that mean it's still there?"

"Yep. There and just as pretty as ever."

They pulled up in front of the hotel, and Mark leaned across her to open her door. With a devilish look in his eye, he said, "Next time I take you out, will you try to stay sober?" Mary didn't bother to answer him. Thankfully, she made it from the lobby to the elevator without being spotted. She was a mess, and anyone who saw her would have assumed she had the kind of night she wanted to have.

When she checked her telephone, she had a message from Kate that said the circus thing hadn't worked out because one of the elephants was jealous of her, so she had joined a head-banger band, bleached and permed her hair, and changed her blue contacts to purple. She thought she heard her nieces' laughter in the background, and guessed that the whole family was together for dinner.

Beached

Mary looked at the palm tree swaying outside her lanai and stumbled backwards far enough to hang a *Do Not Disturb* sign on her door. Then she crawled between her sheets and said a prayer to the gods of nausea, headaches, and sunburn.

When she awoke hours later, the first thing she spotted was the little cardboard sign that said *Harvest Joy* she put on her nightstand. Am I harvesting joy, Mary asked herself, or am I harvesting trouble? No, she decided, it really, truly, was a harvest of joy. She gave herself a lot of points for going out with a man and meeting new people. It hadn't turned out to be a romantic evening, but that wasn't her fault. Mark was the one who pulled back; she was ready. She reached for her pen and entered her activity in her journal. She didn't go into details; this journal was more of an activity journal than a tell-all diary. Mary was tracking her path back to what she called the living and, in her mind, any comparison of her to a ghostly body rising from a dank grave was fully intentional.

When she returned her notebook to the bed table, she noticed the red light flashing on her phone, but she ignored it and rolled over and went back to sleep. *Had the phone been ringing? Did she care?*

She didn't hear the phone when it rang, but she heard a firm fist beating on her door right after she'd gone back to sleep. Mark's voice kept calling her name over and over. "Mary! Open the door! Come on, Mary, wake up. Maaaarrrry!"

When Mary stumbled to the door, she expected to see a cheerful guy holding a paper sack full of food, announcing a picnic. What she saw was a sad face holding a gym bag with an airline ticket in his pocket. In his other hand, he was juggling two cups of Kona coffee and condiments in a little paper sack. Mary took the coffee to the table on the lanai and watched as Mark dropped his gym bag and a sack loaded with hastily purchased gifts on her bed.

"Mark? What's happened?"

"Mary, Mom called. Linda has quit her job and run off with some guy who wants to raise emus in Okanogan. She dumped the girls at Mom's and Karen is so upset it triggered her asthma attacks. I've got to go back."

"Oh, no, Mark. Where did Linda meet this guy?"

"The girls say she met him at some singles' party that was being held on a ferry out on Puget Sound."

"What about her job?"

"Doesn't need one, she says. These emus are going to make them both rich, then she says she'll send for the girls."

"When?"

"In a year or two. Mom says the girls can finish out their school year with her, then spend the summer with me. With anything involving Linda, there's no use in planning beyond that. I've got to go back and get them settled down and see about Karen's asthma."

"How's your mom doing?"

"She's mad as hell. Says this guy's a real loser and the girls told her he has a car trunk full of brochures from all sorts of businesses, all of them with his name on them."

"What is Linda thinking?"

"I'm guessing he got her attention when he said they'd be rich. Linda has been looking for a rich husband since the divorce. I never did make enough to keep her satisfied."

"How soon does your plane leave?"

"I'm on standby for the 2:00 flight, I've got to leave right away." Mark pulled Mary to him and held her tight. "I don't like leaving you, especially when you're having doubts about us because I don't have any. I was hoping I could seal the deal while we were here."

"I wish I could feel as sure about us as you do, but Mark, whatever happens, I'll always want what's best for you and the girls, you know that. If they need a place to stay at any time, you know they're welcome with Kate and me."

"Thanks. I don't know what I'm going to do. Amy is going to graduate this year, and I hate to change her school again. Karen's asthma really acted up the last time she had to change schools. She's being treated at the University Hospital, and she's comfortable with the doctors there; I can't change her treatment while she's so upset. But for right now, they're at Mom's, and she seems to be tickled to have them. She even went out and bought one of those hot air popcorn machines for our girls. It's one big slumber party over there."

Mary was surprised. *Elizabeth had purchased a popcorn machine?* "Do you have five minutes to hug an old friend?"

Mark checked his watch and said, "I can give you six minutes of uninterrupted hugging. I'm so sorry about this Mary. If we'd married each other instead of the dummies we fell for, we wouldn't be having these problems."

"I think you're right. But then again, maybe one of us would still develop a fondness for emus."

"That would never happen with us. Besides, I've been checking things out here on the islands. Do you know that it's a law here that if you see a girl's boobies while she's in your sleeping bag, she has to marry you?"

Mary almost doubled over in embarrassment; in the excitement, she'd forgotten all about the sleeping bag slipping off of her when Mark came into the tent. "Relax," Mark laughed, "I've been admiring your figure for years, the thing with the sleeping bag was nothing more than a confirmation that everything's there, and in good shape, too." Mary tried to look away, but Mark cradled her face between his hands and forced her to look into his eyes. "No more games between us, Mary. I know you have reservations about rejoining my family, but we can work it out." He cupped his hand over a breast and held it there while he kissed her long and strong. Mary didn't resist. She took advantage of every minute and leaned into Mark's body, and savored his response to her closeness.

Mark left for the airport and Mary sipped her cold coffee on the lanai. She'd never see those crazy rangers again. Where were they now? Probably finishing off the spiked fruit drink and spreading the leftover poi on the fishing waters. She looked over at her journal but ignored it. She just wanted to sit and feel the aftershocks of a relationship that was being kicked into high gear before she was ready. There was a soft knock at the door, but Mark was gone, so it most likely was housekeeping. She grabbed her sandals and her wallet, ready to vacate the room so the women in peach-colored uniforms could do their magic. When she opened the door, instead of housekeeping, she found a bellboy holding a hat woven out of palm fronds, and covered in plastic fruit. Sensing the mood was not joyous, the young man offered the hat at arm's length, and said, "I'm supposed to tell you that Mark said for you to be sure and wear this." Mary tried to smile. She'd seen the hats at the hotel gift shop, and pictured Mark tearing through the crowded display trying to find another way to say he was sorry. Her eyes filled with water, and when she looked up, the bellboy was gone. She pulled the hat onto her head and moved in front of the mirror. It wasn't her best look. She put the hat on backwards, over her face. There. That was better.

Can I do that?

To avoid a fifteen dollar hamburger from the hotel restaurant, Mary lived off her fruit from Mark—the real fruit he'd left for her at the hotel desk. She didn't remember that someone had taken a picture of her and Mark until she discovered it in the outside pocket of her beach bag. She noticed the dress looked darn good, even with a grass skirt wrapped around it. She stared at the photo until it was too dark on the lanai to see it, then she stared anyway, not needing to see it to feel what it was.

Back and forth, she walked between the lanai and her room, all the time holding the photo in her hand. Before she went to bed, she placed the promise of the rest of her life over the *Harvest Joy* sign. That is, if she could get over her reservations about re-entering Mark's family. What made Mark so sure she could? He was asking her to come up with a different answer to her problems when the facts were the same. No matter how they felt about each other, she would still be a Bergstrom again, along with all of the stress and doubts that went along with the name. The fact that she was dragging Mark around with her in her circle of doubt didn't make her feel any better. The poor guy deserved a lot better than he was getting from her.

The first time she'd ever seen him, he'd just gotten out of the army and had his new bride by his side. Mary was already married to Brian, and both of the men were wrapped up in starting their families and careers. Right away, Mark was hired by the Montana Park System, and he and Linda took off to live in a little park cabin. Mary barely saw them. There was never a closeness between the brothers, but it took Mary years to figure out why: Brian was a scoundrel; Mark wasn't. The two couldn't have had less in common if they'd been born to separate parents. Now, years later, the rift between them had grown deeper.

Mark never let on about his brother; Mary finally figured it out for herself. She found herself alone much of the time. After Kate's birth, it wasn't just the physical distance that separated them when Brian was away, but the distance between their hearts grew with every suspicion Mary had of her husband's affairs. With no actual proof, and a growing daughter who adored her father, Mary had talked herself into letting their problems slide. Maybe, she kept telling herself, things would get better. They didn't. It never occurred to her that Mark was also unhappy. She had little contact with her sister-in-law, and Mark had never said anything against Linda. Mary never dreamed that she would someday look at Mark and see more than a brother-in-law. And now, here she was, on an island vacation all alone with a straw hat covered in plastic fruit given to her by a man she'd never thought of in a romantic way, and now desperately wanted.

Still feeling totally unhinged the next day, she decided to make a list and go on a forced march. She could get her shopping done, check on her departure tickets, and look for her friends. She was leaving on Sunday, and that left her the rest of the day and one more. If she got everything organized, she could take a shuttle out to Hanauma Bay, and snorkel in the underwater park. She wasn't really in the mood for snorkeling, but she paid good money for this trip, and who knew when she'd be back?

She was leaving her room when the phone rang. She'd never been so surprised or delighted to hear from anyone in her life. Delighted because it was Mark, and surprised because her ex had never called her when he was out of town except to get a brief report of household events. Here, Mary had a man who was calling to ask about *her*.

"How are your girls?" Mary asked.

"They're settling down, Kate's helping a lot, Mary. You know, Karen looks up to her." Mark paused and took a breath. "Mary, I have something to tell you. My flight was delayed for forty-five minutes, but I didn't want to call you and get you all upset again."

"That's okay, I understand."

"That's not what I have to tell you. I bought you a ring at the airport gift shop. Now, I know you're not convinced you want to take that step yet, but this is a Hawaiian flower ring. I figured it would be all right if you thought of it as a friendship ring." The other end of the line was silent. "Mary?"

"Mark, you take my breath away," Mary finally said.

"Will you wear it? Please say yes."

"Mark, we're moving too fast, but I have to tell you that I want that ring more than I've ever wanted anything, and I *will* wear it."

"Good, because I bought three of them. I wasn't sure what size your finger was."

"I'll wear them all, Smokey, just to be sure you're not spreading them around."

"Are you still mad at me for not making love to you at the luau?" he asked softly.

"No, just sad. I feel very, very, sad, Mark. Like we may be two ships that passed in the night, never to be that close again."

"We're not going to be like that. We're going to be like the two Douglas firs in front of my ranger cabin in Montana, so close you can't get a stick between them, their branches intertwining all the way to their tops." Mark took a breath, "Look, Mary, we're both adults. Let's act like it. See if you can get an early flight on Sunday, and I'll pick you up and we'll spend some time together before you go home. No one will be the wiser."

"Can I do that?"

"Call and see. I'll call you back in forty-five minutes to get the details on your arrival."

Mary called the airline and was surprised at how easy it was. "Is your car at the airport?" Mark asked when he called. "No, it's at the house. You can drop me off and I can drive to your mom's from there to pick up Kate. Mark, is this going to work?"

"Sure it is. We're not jinxed. We're just two nice people who need a break. See you Sunday morning."

Snorkeling would have to wait. Mary raced out of the hotel to get her shopping done. She found a beach tote for Roxanne, a straw mat for Ray, and a shorts set for Elizabeth from the same shop that sold her the muumuu. For her ex-father-in-law, an avid griller, she picked up a set of Hawaiian teriyaki sauces in ginger and pineapple flavorings. She looked for something for Mark and almost came up empty, until she saw a little hula girl in a grass skirt to go on the dash of his forest service vehicle. For Kate's cousins, she picked up necklace and earring sets made from tiny seashells. She got a small box of Hawaiian chocolates with macadamia nuts for Brian, not because she cared, but because she wanted to make sure he knew she'd been to Hawaii. In the shops, she saw flower rings carved from mother-of-pearl, and smiled; the rings were inexpensive, but sweet. She couldn't wait for Mark to give her hers. Her shopping done, Mary raced back to her hotel room to check for messages. Before she got on the plane, she would pick-up a six-pack of fresh pineapple that Elizabeth had asked for. They always had stacks of it, boxed up and ready to go at the airport.

Back in her room, Mary had another message from Kate that said she and her cousins had decided to get dreadlocks, and hitchhike to the Caribbean. Grandmother had gotten her hair done too so she could go with them. They figured they could find a reggae band and sign on as groupies. They would take the popcorn machine with them.

10
That's a big earthquake!

As she was leaving her last shop, she ran into her friends, who were getting ready to fly out that evening and wanted to take her to the hotel bar that served mai-tais in a pineapple shell. Mary accepted readily.

She gave her friends a quick idea of the luau. Their mouths watered when she described the picnic table loaded with exotic food. Mary agreed it was wonderful, but it was a long time ago. She ordered an assortment of special Hawaiian appetizers for all of them to go with the drinks. She hadn't had a real meal since Mark had filled her plate.

The women hung on every word that left Mary's lips and relished every detail about her romantic evening. They even saw something positive about her unplanned exposure in the tent: "Ya gotta let the guy verify the jewels, Hon," Marge cackled. "Believe me, he must have been so surprised that he won't soon forget 'em!" Mary had never had the nerve to ask Mark if he had undressed her in the tent, so she wasn't sure if he was surprised or not. *Oh, she hoped he was.*

While Lucille recounted a story about how her future husband had accidentally walked in on her when she was nude right after they'd first met, Mary shared her appetizers with the women. Stuffed mushrooms filled with cheese, teriyaki chicken, coconut shrimp, and barbecued pork filled an oval platter decorated with grilled pineapple slices. The pork wasn't as good as the pork Halo had brought, but it was a good substitute. After her first drink, she told the girls she had reached her limit so she could be sure all of the alcohol was out of her system when she met Mark in Seattle. It wasn't like her to drink so much. She blamed it on all of the drinks being mixed with fruit juice. In this climate, who wouldn't want an icy drink that tasted like coconut, papaya, pineapple, or mango?

"…and there I was, in the kitchen unloading the dishwasher without a stitch on when the earthquake hit," Lucille laughed as she ended her story.

"So what happened then?" Jean asked.

"Let's just say the earth kept moving—all night long."

"How big was it?" Marge asked.

Without missing a step, Lucille replied, "Oh, it was about 9.9 or so."

When Marge said, "That's a big earthquake!"

Lucille acted surprised. "Oh, *that*? I dunno. I never heard."

The women all laughed. To soon, they had to get going. Jean was especially anxious to get home. She missed her husband. All of the women suspected he was on some sort of secret woodworking project because he seldom answered the phone. Jean told Mary he couldn't hear the phone ring when his wood saw was running. There was a flurry of goodbyes as they each gathered up their packages. Their luggage was already in the lobby, so Mary said goodbye to the women outside the bar, underneath the sea shell lamp where they'd first met. "Email me, my address is in the magazine," Mary called as she waved goodbye.

Her message light was blinking on her phone when she got back to her room. She found a final message from Kate that said they'd taken a side trip to Cuba, and Castro had spotted their grandmother on the beach. Instantly smitten with her, he'd taken them all back to his villa to live with him forever. She'd write.

Mary smiled. She could detect some stress in Kate's message, but no panic. Elizabeth had everything under control.

11
A song of goodbye

The next day, Mary was embarrassed to say, time dragged. How could anyone be on a tropical paradise and not have time fly by? She had to force herself to get her act together and take the shuttle to Hanauma Bay to go snorkeling. She was exhausted when she hit the water, and it must have showed. A fellow swimmer warned her to stay clear of the area known as the Toilet Bowl, where the swimming was a lot harder due to the huge amount of water that flushed through the rocks there. When she looked where the man pointed, she noticed that the bulk of the swimmers playing in the explosive and powerful waves there were much younger, and undoubtedly stronger. She took the man's advice, and kept closer to shore where the snorkeling was pleasant and easy. She didn't feel a bit cheated. Never had she seen so many fish. Mary had gotten smart, and worn a tee-shirt to protect her shoulders from the sun. She had a feeling it was too little too late, but she was glad she had when she was still there in late afternoon.

She spent so much time snorkeling that she never did make it to The Bishop Museum, founded by Princess Pauahi to hold all of her artifacts on Hawaiian life and culture. It was just as well. Her brochure said that The Bishop was constantly growing, and was packed with over 20 million acquisitions. It definitely deserved its own day.

Unfortunately, the next day didn't see Mary on the shuttle for the famous museum. She was too exhausted from snorkeling all day the day before, and too emotionally keyed up to appreciate the artifacts that would be on display there. After a few false starts, she admitted to herself that the museum and all its treasures would have to wait until the next trip. She was destined to spend the rest of her time in Hawaii on her lanai with her journal.

She also wondered what Linda was up to. Mary and her mother-in-law had never been close, but she had no doubt that Elizabeth was handling the situation with Linda as well or better than anyone else could. And there was never any question of her love for her grandchildren. Mary shook her head. Elizabeth had signed up for a few days with Kate and had ended up being in the middle of a family disaster. She was glad she'd purchased a nice gift for her. She had never gotten many phone calls from Elizabeth, but she was surprised that Elizabeth hadn't called her about Mark's situation. After all, the ongoing events impacted Kate. Maybe her mother-in-law needed her there to help calm the girls. Mary tried to ignore the other possibility that Elizabeth hadn't called her because she didn't consider the situation to be any of her business, since Brian had divorced her. She hoped that wasn't it.

Mark hadn't called her, but she was sure it was because he had his hands full with his girls and his ex-wife. Mary packed most of her carry-on before she went to bed, and left the little pink silk chemise she'd purchased at the muumuu shop on top. A quick jump through the shower to wash off the latest batch of dead, over-tanned skin was the extent of her evening's entertainment. Unmindful of cost, Mary celebrated her last night in Hawaii on the lanai with a can of soda from her refrigerator. She heard that anything taken from those little refrigerators cost more than a down payment on a beach house, but she didn't want to leave her room to run down to the pop machines at the end of the hall and chance a missed call from Mark. While Mary drank her pop, the little dove, already nestled behind the potted plant in the corner, cooed a song of goodbye. It was after one when Mary turned out the lights to go to sleep. Five minutes later, they went back on. *Who was she kidding? There would be no sleep tonight.* Excitement ran through her body and left her eyes wide open and her hands shaking. Was she really going to go to bed with Mark? *Yes, she was.* Was it the smart thing to do? *Maybe not!* Her flight instinct took hold, and she raced around the room, her brain on fast forward. *Was she ready to become a part of that family again? Was she nuts? Would she be happy to be the low man on the totem pole for the rest of her life?* Her brain skipped over the part where she could consider giving up Mark. She couldn't do that. But maybe she wouldn't have to marry him. *Yeah, right. Look who's talking. The woman who has been divorced for two years and never done a sleepover, as Roxanne called them.*

While Mary had her panic attack, she repacked her suitcase again. And brushed her teeth *again.* She woke up the dove on the lanai when she pulled her chair over to the creature and asked her—Mary was sure she was female—for advice. Mama bird just blinked her eyes and cooed.

On the street twelve floors below, it was quieting down. Only a few old men sat at picnic tables in the sand strip between the street and the surf to play cards. She guessed it was too hot in their rooms to sleep. She watched them for awhile; they were so comfortable with their everyday life on an island that tourists were lucky just to visit for a few days. It was like they were in a separate dimension, and they couldn't see the visitors criss-crossing the sand around them. Mary's time on their island wasn't anything like theirs, but it had turned out much better than she'd hoped, even though it had a few glitches. Like a man, something Mary swore she didn't want, but had now decided she did. With a moneyed family she didn't want that would constantly put pressure on her to keep up. At least she'd feel that way. Mary wasn't worried about Kate fitting back into her father's family. She was young, and had absorbed a lot of the Bergstrom's moxie. She had to face it: for her, the only perk in this arrangement would be Mark. And Mark's girls. Kate had always wanted sisters. She and Kate were both fond of their brother, John, but he was in college, and was going to school on the east coast. It was impossible to tell where he'd settle down.

The night almost over, Mary put her suitcase and purse by the door and pulled a short crocheted sweater over her tank top. She checked her hair and makeup and decided to wait until just before she landed at Sea-Tac to redo it. With any luck, she'd sleep on the plane.

Although she'd already checked out at the desk, she stopped to visit with the cashier and thank him for his hotel's gracious services. Even though she would have liked to suggest the management post a sign warning swimmers about the window at the bottom of the hotel pool, she couldn't bring herself to mention the incident with the scrunchie. Partly, because she was afraid the employee would laugh and say, "Oh, was that *you?*" She went out the door to get on the shuttle for the airport, and turned one more time to look at the flowering hibiscus in the courtyard, just to make sure there weren't any bears.

At last!

Mary did sleep on the plane. She awoke just in time to run a brush through her hair and adjust her makeup. Loaded down with her carry-on and the sack of gifts that didn't fit inside, she was entering the terminal in the Sea-Tac Airport when she remembered that Elizabeth had asked for a box of fresh pineapple. She felt a slight twinge in her chest; once again, she'd failed to measure up.

Mark's was the first face she saw. He took her breath away with his open smile and welcoming arms. As she fell into his embrace he easily took over the overnight bag and packages she was carrying. "I forgot your mother's pineapple," Mary mumbled as she looked into his eyes.

"That's okay. I bought three boxes." Looking around quickly, he picked an escape route through the crowd. "Let's get out of here. Hold onto my shirt so I don't lose you." Off they went, breaking a trail through the maze of high-spirited people with skins shades darker than they were when they left.

Quickly, they opened the backdoor to Mark's rental car on the passenger side and tossed in all of Mary's baggage. With his hands finally free, he threw his arms around Mary and bent down to kiss her lips. His voice was rough when he said, "I'm so glad we decided to do this. I got us a room at the new hotel across the street; we'll be there in five minutes." While they were stopped at a red light, he added, "Mary, I don't want you to think I've been sleeping around, but I bought us some protection. I know you and I wouldn't need it, but we have no idea who our ex-spouses have been with."

"I think that was smart. Thanks." Mary sat back in the seat and casually hooked her seatbelt. All the jitters from the night before were gone. Who could be nervous looking into that joyous face with the open smile and twinkling blue eyes?

In their hotel room, Mark was like a kid. "Check out the shower! It's supposed to be like a rain forest, and it's huge!" Then he kidded, "Of course, we can't use it. With Seattle's water shortage, hundreds of fish must die when anyone showers in there. You'll have to use the sink."

Mary suddenly noticed she smelled like the inside of an airplane. On her way to the shower she stopped by her suitcase to grab the silk negligee. It would be on for less than a minute, but Mary was counting on it to get her from the bathroom to the bed. It had been a long time since a man had seen her totally naked.

She needn't have bothered. She was beginning to rinse out her hair when she looked up to see Mark stepping under the rain shower with her. At the sight of him—all of him—she shivered and began to cry. Puzzled, Mark asked, "Mary, you're not afraid of me are you?"

"No," Mary assured him. "It's just been a long time." She moved into his arms and the two stood there for awhile, letting the warm water rain on their shoulders and run down the outside of their bodies. He easily lifted her up onto a tiled ornamental column that stood in the middle of the shower and wrapped her legs around his waist. While he kissed her, he caressed her hair, heavy with shampoo, and gently pulled it off her face before his hands moved over her wet, slippery breasts. Eagerly, they followed the path of the water all the way to the spot between her legs where the water collected in a tiny v-shaped pool. He explored the secret cave gently with his fingers as Mary groaned with desire. Then he entered her. The soft rain of the shower wrapped them in a steamy fog. He moved slowly and tenderly at first, then plunged himself deeply into Mary as she urged him to finish. When Mark began to caress her again and then re-entered her, Mary gasped with surprise. Love-making with Brian had never been like this. A virgin when she'd married, she'd never considered that Brian might not be good at sex. She had nothing to compare him to. Now, with Mark, she discovered what love-making really was, and she held onto him and pulled him as close to her as possible. She'd never let him go.

By the time Mark lifted her out of the shower and wrapped a towel around her body, the pink silk negligee on the hook behind the bathroom door was forgotten. When he laid her on the bed, he stood there, unsure of himself. When Mary asked him what was wrong, he explained, "Times have changed since I last dated. I just remembered that I was supposed to ask you if you wanted me to stop."

Mary pulled his hand gently to her breast. "Come to bed. We'll figure out the new rules later."

The next too-short hours were filled with love, passion, and laughter. At sometime during their lovemaking, Mark slipped the flower ring on Mary's finger; its beauty made her gasp. It had been seriously undersold. Mary had assumed the ring was like the shell rings she'd seen in the gift shops. This ring was a hibiscus flower in 14K gold. The dainty curves of the ring's design were accented by three tiny diamonds set into the center of the golden flower. This was a serious ring from a serious man, and Mary was enchanted.

13

A green finger

Several hours later, they loaded their suitcases and memories into Mark's rental car. When they got to Mary's house, they suddenly felt nervous about getting caught. They both went through their sacks to make sure their purchases hadn't found their way into the wrong bag, although neither of them remembered looking in the bags.

"Mark, what shall we do about the ring? No one will believe I bought it for myself."

"You're right. It could be a problem. Could you move it to your right hand? That might help."

"I can, but it still looks way too good for my budget."

"Well, we could get married on the way to Mom's," Mark presented his solution with his best Groucho Marx impression, wiggling his eyebrows and pretending he had a cigar.

Mary laughed, "I don't think I'm ready to make an announcement yet. I guess I'll have to take it off for now. I hate to."

"It won't be for long. I'm not going to let this charade go on forever. The rest of the family will go along with us, or not. But I would like for the girls to be settled and calm before we spring something else on them."

"I agree. I'm not even sure Kate is ready for us to be a couple yet. She's already absorbing the emotional trauma of her dad's date-of-the-week."

After Mark left, she decided to wear the ring a little while longer so she could look at it as she drove to his parents' home. Sometime during the ride, the ring became a part of her.

A part of her and Mark.
A part of the new Mary.
She completely forgot she had it on.

* * *

Mark beat Mary to his parent's house and she pulled her car right behind his rental. By agreement, he wasn't there. At Mary's request, as soon as he'd arrived, he'd herded the girls to his house on the family compound so they could swim in his backyard pool. She was feeling nervous about facing his mother, and she thought it'd be easier if he weren't there at first.

When she went into the house, she could barely hear the television in the entertainment room at the back of the house, but the noise in the kitchen left no doubt that Elizabeth was busy making a big meal. It wasn't often she had a full house for dinner anymore, and she had every burner on the stove going.

"Smells good in here," Mary said to Mark's mother.

"Mary! I'm sorry we couldn't meet your plane, dear. I got tied up with cooking and Mark couldn't make it to pick up the girls."

"That's okay. I had my car there anyway. No use in everyone being on the freeway. How are the girls?"

"Did Kate tell you Linda left?" Mary nodded no, and Elizabeth told her the whole story. "I couldn't bear to call you and tell you. Kate and I agreed there was nothing you could do about it anyway. The girls are better now. They fell apart when their mom dumped them off here, and then, they had the added shock of realizing they would have to leave their friends and change schools again, for a second time. Kate was a big help, Mary. I'm so glad she was here." She handed Mary a glass of iced tea and pointed toward the family room. "We've got two men in the den watching the game and Mark has the girls in his pool."

Mary had expected her ex-father-in-law to be home, but she hadn't expected Kate's father to be there too. She hadn't noticed Brian's car in the driveway; maybe it was at the back of the house. She said a quick hello to the men watching television and retreated back to the kitchen.

"How was Hawaii?" Elizabeth asked.

"So good I hated to leave."

"I didn't realize Mark was going to be there at the same time. I don't suppose you ran into him?"

"No," Mary said with a laugh, "It's a pretty big place. What was he doing there?"

"Oh, it was some kind of park ranger convention, I guess."

Mary was relieved when she couldn't detect any suspicion in Elizabeth's voice. There was a clamor at the backdoor and all of the girls, followed by Mark, came into the kitchen. Mary held her breath and forced herself to look at the man she was pretending she didn't have any interest in. Mark beamed back at her and winked. She almost fell off her chair. A quick scan of the kitchen told her no one else had seen it. "I thought you were swimming?" Mary asked when she noticed everyone was dry and dressed.

"We were, but I wanted to come and see you so we cut it short. We got dressed at Uncle Mark's," Kate explained, "so we wouldn't drip all over grandmother's floors.

"Besides," Karen chimed in, "we didn't think she'd let us into her dining room with wet swimsuits and we're hungry!"

Mary hugged Kate. "I missed you. Have you been good?"

"Yes, except for that spray paint we decorated dad's new yacht with."

"New yacht? I didn't notice a new boat at the dock."

"It's not here yet. It's too big to fit right now. The slip isn't big enough. He took us to the marina to see it. It's huge, Mom. We went for a spin around the sound to break it in."

Mary detected some stress on Elizabeth's face, but nothing was said. *A yacht. A big one. Well, Elizabeth and Fred would never have to worry about Mary and Mark needing a bigger slip.*

Slip. Mary's face reddened when she remembered the pink nightie she'd left hanging behind the bathroom door at the hotel. Drat! She'd be too embarrassed to go and ask for it; it was lost forever. Thank goodness Elizabeth would never know. Mary was continually fighting the feeling that she didn't measure up, and this would be just another example of her incompetence. She didn't dare to consider how Elizabeth would feel if she knew Mary and Mark had started a relationship.

Mark, on the other hand, didn't have any concerns about how his parents would feel about the decisions he made. He had emotional ties to his family, but no financial obligations. He was free to live his own life. Brian could live his. If his brother had a newer, bigger yacht, that was fine with him. It wasn't that he disliked money, he just didn't feel that he needed piles of it to be comfortable. He'd kept a house on the family compound not for the status but so his girls could be close to their grandparents when they visited. Then he'd built the pool to keep them out of the saltwater that was deep and black where they were. He much preferred the lake water in Montana that was clear all the way to the bottom. It was a known fact that the largest octopus in the world were in Puget Sound. Some were known to get as large as twelve to fourteen feet across. Not being able to see what could be in the water, swimming with his girls, made Mark more than uneasy. It scared the heck out of him.

"What was wrong with the old yacht?" Mary asked no one in particular.

"My big brother is courting the Saudis," Mark explained. "He says they never go anywhere alone. They always travel in an entourage, so he needs room for all of them."

Another pained expression passed Elizabeth's face; again, she said nothing.

"Will someone go and tell the men watching the game that we're ready to eat?" Elizabeth asked. "The rest of you girls can start carrying the crab platters and clams to the table. There's salad and bread on the counter too." Elizabeth looked at Mary and asked, "Did you bring any pineapple, Mary? I hope not because Mark brought a bunch of it."

"I'm sorry, I forgot the pineapple, Elizabeth, but I did bring you something else."

"Then you're forgiven," Elizabeth said with a smile. "And don't forget to take some pineapple home with you when you go. The girls sliced up enough to fill a big platter and there's still two boxes leftover. I may have to freeze some of it."

Too late, it was discovered that Mark's girls had unconsciously set a place at the table for Linda. Elizabeth was surprised and frozen into inaction. Should she remove the plate? Leave it? A quiet sadness fell over the table. After a few uncomfortable moments, Kate decided that, if they left the place setting at the table, it would just worsen the situation. She eased out of her chair and took the extra setting to the kitchen. On her way around the table, she paused to give her cousins a sympathetic hug. Elizabeth gave Kate a grateful smile for handling the crisis so delicately when she came back from the kitchen. She'd been through some long days with her granddaughters, and she was too exhausted to think.

Even Brian felt badly for the girls, and started babbling about his plans for the yacht, and how it was going to increase business. Mark jumped in with tales of his crazy Hawaiian rangers, and fishing with rancid poi. Mary added her stories of the women she'd met from Grand Forks who showed her where the bargains were. Before long, the cloud over the table lifted, and the girls relaxed.

They were sitting at the table happily devouring seafood and tossing the empty shells into a big bowl in the middle when Kate, from the other side of the table, loudly said, "Mom, that's a killer ring! Is it real?"

Mary dropped her crab cracker and was about to slip under the table when Mark came to her rescue. "I saw those rings all over Waikiki. "Don't get it wet, sis, unless you want a green finger."

Right after a dessert of strawberry shortcake that the girls had made, before anyone had time to put two and two together, Mary and Mark passed out the presents they'd brought, and Mary took Kate home. The ring and the pineapple seemed to be forgotten.

14

Linda's emu farm

On the way home that night, Kate talked and talked until Mary thought there couldn't possibly be anymore, but then her daughter would take a breath and start in again. Most of her conversation was about the emus Kate and her cousins had researched on the Internet. "Mom, did you know that kangaroos and emus can't walk backwards?"

Mary laughed. "No, Kate, that information has never come up on my computer screen."

The girls also determined that Linda was making the biggest mistake of her life. The emu market was just a fad; everyone else in the business was trying to get out. Worse, they were sure that the new man Kate's cousins' mother was so in love with was not only a big loser, but an alcoholic. Kate confided that she was sure the man was only after her cousins' money.

"What money?" Mary asked.

"The money Uncle Mark put in the college fund for my cousins after Aunt Linda divorced him."

Mary was surprised to hear Kate mention the college money. Kate had a similar fund. Elizabeth insisted upon a fund being set aside for her granddaughters so that they would be okay, no matter what crazy thing their parents did. But Mary was sure that no money could be withdrawn without two signatures. At least, she hoped her memory was correct. She'd ask Mark about it as soon as possible. At the time, neither of the sons had enough money to establish a trust fund to ensure the girls' educations, so their parents had added a big chunk of money, at Elizabeth's insistence. As far as Mary knew, her ex-mother-in-law had no interest in pouring her money into an emu farm.

The next morning, there was a message from Mark on Mary's phone at work. She smiled as he asked, "Well, that went well, didn't it? Has your finger turned green yet?" he went on to say that shortly, he and the girls would be on their way to Seattle to see Karen's asthma specialist and he'd call her after he talked to her doctor.

She was still smiling when Roxanne and Ray came into the office loaded down with cups of coffee from a different shop. "What's this? No Wizard's?" Mary asked.

One look at Ray's face told the story. Sadly, he filled in the details for Mary. It seemed that his new love had found another and had dumped Ray in a voicemail. He hadn't even bothered to tell him in person. Ray was guessing his ex-lover's new guy was a banker, from the looks of him. The new coffee shop of choice was Lotta's, just down the street from The Seattle Art Museum. Mary hadn't been there, but she'd read in the paper that the walls had huge reproductions of black artist Jacob Lawrence's paintings on its walls. From what she'd read, the ambiance the colorful paintings created made the coffee shop an overnight success with the art crowd. The new coffee bar wasn't as close as Wizard's, but no one from the office wanted to go back there now.

Mary couldn't think of anything to say to Ray except that he would find someone better. It was obvious the barista wasn't good enough for him; anyone who would leave someone over the telephone wasn't a keeper. Out of words and ideas at the same time, Mary quickly passed out the gifts she'd brought for them and everyone pretended to go back to work. Mary stared at a website from Hawaii that had a live feed of the Waikiki beach. Actually, it was a traffic-cam, but someone had turned the camera toward the water. Roxanne was checking the community calendar for places where Captain Marvelous, her name for her future husband, might be hanging out, and Ray was stringing a box of a thousand colored paper clips into a chain. He said it could take hours to complete, but he was no quitter.

Later, at lunch, Roxanne quickly filled Mary in on the details Ray had left out. The barista had actually tried to borrow money, a lot of it, before he dumped Ray. The only reason Ray didn't give it to him was because he didn't have that much; the guy had wanted a down payment for a BMW. They agreed that Ray had a close call. He was brokenhearted, but, at least, the greedy so-and-so hadn't cleaned out his bank account.

Mary was in no mood for Roxanne's disapproval when her friend asked her about her trip, so she focused mainly on the women she'd met, and the disaster at the pool the first night she was there. Mark, she told Roxanne, had to leave early because of his ex-wife's infatuation with emus that had brought on Karen's asthma attack. They'd barely had time to say hello, she told her friend.

"What are you doing for the rest of the day?" she asked Mary.

"I'm way ahead on my stories, so I'll probably work on the story about Northwest artists. I'm hoping it'll be the cover story." Mary added, "I've sent a request to legal to see if we can get permission from the artists. I'm hoping they will all agree that being on the cover of *Sea the Northwest* will be good for all of us."

Actually, the story was almost finished. The cover, if they could do it, would be so gorgeous that it would blow all of the other magazines off the rack at the newsstands. The other choices, a cover with a pet cemetery with its plastic tombstones or a photo of a giant, spitting Palouse earthworm over three feet long, made Mary shudder. The worms, thought to be extinct, had been recently rediscovered in more than one location in Washington State. One of her other stories, a piece about the Kennewick

Man, had already been rejected as a cover story because the editors feared a cover photo of a 9,000 year-old-skeleton discovered on the banks of the Columbia River would make the magazine look like an archaeology magazine. Mary had to agree, although the struggle between the Indians and scientists over ownership of the skeleton made a good story. She was glad the stories were almost finished because it would be hard to concentrate on work until she talked to Mark about Linda's plan to use his girls' college money to fund her new emu ranch. Of course, Mary told herself on her way back to her desk, if she really got hard up for a cover story, there was always Linda's emu ranch, but by the time it came out, Linda could be in jail. *That's not funny,* Mary scolded herself. *Would it be funny if Ray had said it first? Probably not.*

Her phone was ringing when she got back to her desk. It was Elizabeth. "Mary, dear, I'm sorry to bother you at work, but I can't get a hold of Mark. I think he turned his cell phone off when he took Karen to the doctor and forgot to turn it back on."

"That's okay, Elizabeth, you can call me anytime. Is something wrong?"

"Well, I don't know. Someone from the bank called to say that someone was trying to withdraw money from Amy and Karen's trust fund, and I'm sure Mark would have told me if he was going to do anything like that. Besides, he knows there has to be two signatures to make a withdrawal."

Linda was moving fast. "How much money did they try to withdraw?"

"All of it. For both girls."

"It's getting late," Mary told Elizabeth. "Mark must be stuck in traffic. Did you put a freeze on the funds until you talk to him?"

"I should have, but to tell you the truth, I was so surprised I didn't think. I was annoyed with him for not telling me when we were together last night. I could understand it if it were Brian.

He's always had big ideas, but why would Mark need that much money?"

"Elizabeth, I haven't a clue. It doesn't sound like Mark."

"Fred has an idea it's not Mark at all, but Linda who's behind this. Maybe her new boyfriend tried to pass himself off as Mark. We think it wouldn't be hard for a con artist like him to forge Mark's name."

Mary was relieved when she was able to end the conversation. The longer she talked to Elizabeth, the more danger there was of saying something that would give away her relationship with Mark. Kate and her cousins had been right. Luckily, safeguards had been put into place to prevent unauthorized withdrawals. She didn't think she'd hear from Mark again until the problem with Linda and the trust fund had been resolved.

Family troubles

She was wrong. Mark's rental car was in the driveway when she got home. Kate and her cousins were picking cherries in the backyard to make a pie. The remains of a pizza were on the counter and Mary grabbed a piece on her way to change her clothes. Mark was on the phone and from the look on his face Mary guessed it must be his mother, but when he hung up, he said he'd been talking to Linda. She'd gotten a phone call from Elizabeth and she was afraid she was going to be arrested. Her excuse, Mark said, was that she was doing the girls a favor. The emu market was booming! Mark just shook his head. Linda, he said, had always looked for a quick and easy fortune; she'd never change. Maybe that was why she'd married him. She thought she'd be in the money when she married into such a rich family. Once, he confided, his mother had caught Linda in her walk-in closet, trying on her fur coats. It was probably the beginning of the end, he said, when they'd had a fight about it back at their cabin and he'd told her that, if she wanted a fur coat, the woods were full of them, she just had to pick one and shoot it. Soon after, Linda decided that she was being suffocated by fresh mountain air, and she grabbed the kids and ran for the civilized coast where upscale department stores, gourmet restaurants, and coffee bars on every corner opened their arms to her. She took Mark's charge cards along for the ride.

Now, she'd quit her big city job and was willing to risk everything to move to a farm, mountains away from civilization, to raise emus. Mark said before she hung up, she didn't even asked about Amy and Karen.

While the girls pitted cherries and made pie dough, Mark and Mary slipped out to the sundeck with a glass of wine. "This is nice, isn't it? Mark asked, "Our girls together, chatting away and cooking together. They've always been close."

Mary agreed, "I love the sound of their laughter."

"Someday, we'll be together under one roof all the time."

"How long do you think it'll take to get this problem with Linda straightened out?"

"I've turned it over to Mom and her attorneys," Mark answered. "I think they plan to scare the heck out of her so she'll never try to pull a stunt like this again."

Mark looked at Mary with longing in his eyes. "None of this has anything to do with us. Let's get married on the new company yacht and sail away to Bermuda."

Mary laughed, "That's a wonderful mental picture. Would your brother be our captain?"

"Why not? The yacht is big enough for all of us, I hear."

"What's the deal with that? Your mother grimaces every time the subject of the boat comes up."

"She's mad as hell. He bought the monster over dad's objections. Just signed his name and walked out with it; maybe I should say he floated out with it. The family yacht was mom and dad's first boat, you know. Dad proposed to her on it, and she was very sentimental about it. She would have never sold it." While he talked, he tossed the cherries that were damaged and didn't make it into the pie off the deck to the waiting crows. "Mom suspects he's going to use the new pleasure craft to impress his girlfriends more than he's going to use it for business. My parents say they haven't even researched the Arab market yet. They don't really know if they'll buy wood products from us. Because of shipping costs, it makes more sense for them to buy their wood products from east coast companies."

The girls joined them, and laughed that the pie was so big it might take three days to cook. There was plenty of time to run to the local grocery store and rent a DVD, according to Kate, who was dangling Mary's car keys.

There might have been time for romance after the girls left, but the mood was too gloomy. Instead, Mary put on a pot of coffee. As crazy as she was about Mark, her doubts about getting involved with his family again kept resurfacing. She had a fantasy about her next family being trouble free, and now, with Linda acting up, things were looking even worse. She looked out the kitchen window at Mark. He was pensive. Did he have doubts too, or was it just the problem with Linda that was making him look so worried? For whatever reason, the twinkle had definitely gone out of his eyes. Mary couldn't face more problems. She'd be glad when the girls got back, served the pie, and started the movie.

Mary was right. Mark *was* having second thoughts. During the movie, whenever Mary looked at him, his eyes looked glazed. After the movie was over and Kate and her cousins were packing pie to take to their grandparents, Mark took Mary out onto the sundeck.

"Mary, this is no way to start a marriage. We'd better put our plans on hold until I get this thing with Linda under control." He didn't even look at her when he said, "Let's wait awhile until this mess blows over."

Mary was stunned. And hurt. Later that night, she wasn't even sure if she'd said anything. Or if she'd even nodded. All she could remember was her eyes widened until it felt as if they'd never close again. All along she'd had doubts about their relationship, but she'd never expected to hear Mark have questions. And what did he mean when he said they should wait? How long? Was their love not something that would last, but just a vacation fling that was over, and now regrets were setting in?

16
Things get complicated

When Mark left that night, he dropped off his girls at his mom and dad's and went to return the rental car before he took a flight back to Montana. Before he made it to Sea-Tac Airport, he took a right and kept going. Even if he'd stopped to calculate how much it would cost him to drive all the way to Montana, he would have driven anyway.

He needed to think. He had a lot of decisions to make and he had to make sure they were the right ones, otherwise, he'd just make a big mess of things. First of all, it was obvious to him that he needed to get a job on the west coast, so Mary could keep her job. That was the biggie, and it made his heart ache to think of leaving his job in Montana. He'd been so content there, and his roots to the little park that most people bypassed by on their way to Glacier were deeper than the icy lake that was protected by the park's lush, green firs and their graceful boughs. He tried to tell himself that there were parks on the west coast, but he knew it would never be the same. He didn't think of his position as a park ranger at Teton Lake as a job, but more as a steward-ship. He needed to be there to protect the park from developers. Of course, final decisions about the fate of public lands were made much higher up than Mark, but he and Jackson could have a lot of influence on a lower level. Especially Jackson. His family had a winning combination of history and money when it came to park politics. No way did the two want their beloved park to become just another setting to justify a thick cluster of bead and trinket shops.

Then there were the girls. Karen really needed a settled environment; Kate and Amy would need a comfortable place to finish their high school and move onto college. If they stayed at the park until Mark found another job, the cabin would be crowded for awhile, but the girls would be graduated and gone before permission to add an extra room ever got approved by the state. A crowded cabin didn't worry Mark as much as the other problems. At least, they'd all be together. And, one of the bigger problems, their college, would be mostly paid for, thanks to his mother insisting on the trust accounts for her grandchildren. Still, there would be added expenses. The girls would need clothes, and extra money for food and housing. Of course, wherever he and Mary ended up, the girls would want to fly home for holidays. It was expensive to fly. The dollar signs in Mark's head began to add up.

Then, he had to consider his retirement package. The move from one state to another surely would take a big chunk out of his retirement fund, and he and Mary didn't have a lot of time to rebuild his 401-K account. He wasn't sure how much Mary had, but it couldn't be much because she'd stayed home for so many years to raise Kate. Did she own her house? He didn't know. If they had to sell it, how much would it take to get it ready to put on the market? And then, there was medical coverage for all of them. His brother had kept Kate on his policy, but that would change when he and Mary married. Whichever policy they added Kate to, his or Mary's, it would be a big expense. A million smaller details crossed his mind. For the first time in his life, he regretted not having more money. It put a sour feeling in his stomach to even have to think of financial details when all he wanted to do was be with Mary. Unfortunately, the world turned on money, and he wouldn't be doing her any favors if she had to suffer because he screwed up the financial details.

By the time he'd crossed the Montana line, he had a clear mental list of what he had to do and in what order. The first was the toughest. He had to research Washington State Parks and send out a job application to the state's parks department. Then, he'd start sending out applications to the surrounding states. If Mary couldn't keep her job at *Sea the Northwest*, maybe she could snag a similar one in another city. He cringed when he thought he'd have to move his girls again. They had already been through enough trauma.

While he was waiting for responses, he had to clean the cabin and make it ready for the next guy. All of the buildings had to be ship shape, and the equipment had to be tuned and running perfectly. Luckily, Mark always kept up the maintenance on the buildings and equipment, so there wouldn't be a lot to do. However, bad weather would slow him down if Montana had a colder than normal winter.

The plans he'd made for his visiting rangers at Christmas brought a smile to his face, although his heart was heavy. He'd have one last, big party at Teton Lake before he moved on. His friends were expecting a fantasy Christmas, and he would deliver it to them. He even ordered new bedroom furniture from the *Nisqually Jack Christmas Catalog*. Although they would be sleeping in the bunkhouse, they'd be spending a lot of time in his cabin, and he wanted it to look more like Jackson's. Maybe, if things worked out, Mary could come over too, but he had his doubts about that. The way he'd left her, he doubted if she'd leap at the chance to spend Christmas in Montana. He should have done a better job of explaining his concerns to her. He'd hurt her; undoubtedly, she now thought he was a big loser. And maybe he was. If he couldn't solve their financial challenges, how could they get married? He wasn't counting on any inheritance from his parents. They were getting older, and his brother wanted to take over. It was possible there would be no inheritance money by the time Brian got through with the company.

Back at the park, for days, he thought he'd call Mary as soon as he had some good news, but there was none. Days turned into weeks and, now, Mark was wondering how he could explain his finances to Mary and not make her think he just didn't want to marry her. Everyday, he checked the mail, and thought that if he got a job offer, he could call Mary with the news, but the job applications were a disappointment. The budgets for all state public lands were crunched, and the few parks that had slots to fill were looking for someone with a degree in marine biology. Mark had to admit he barely knew a crab from a squid. After the first letters to parks in Washington State didn't turn up any interest, Mark sent out letters to the park departments in every state on the coast, but the replies took their time trickling in. So far, he hadn't had a nibble. Each batch of rejections sent him back to the computer to search for more places he could apply. The list was getting short.

He never considered his last—very last—option: going to work for his family. He knew nothing about the business, so the only spot he could see for himself there was as his brother's lackey. He couldn't think of a better description of a miserable situation. Not only for himself, but for Mary.

In the meantime, he finished all the cleaning and repairs around the park, and had his bedroom cleared out and ready for his new bedroom furniture. One morning a truck arrived and left several large boxes with Nisqually Jack's on the label. Mark strung all of the pieces for his new bed onto the bedroom floor and scratched his head. The instructions for assembly were in English, Japanese, and French. Mark didn't see a lot of difference between them.

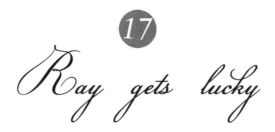

Ray gets lucky

At first, Mary was devastated. Then, she was angry. How could she have been so wrong about a guy? As days flew past with no calls from Mark, the anger turned to sadness. Everyday, she went to work and climbed into her computer. After weeks of silence, she didn't even expect an email message from Montana, and there wasn't one.

She was delighted one day to receive a message from Lucille. She and the girls had come home to another one of George's miracles. While they were gone, he had built a gazebo in his and Jean's backyard, and had planted grape vines around the outside edge to keep it cool. The girls made a big seashell lamp to hang from the center beam. Mary sent the girls a selection of Northwest candies to eat in the new gazebo, along with a note thanking them for their kindnesses.

Mark and Linda's girls were with their grandmother. They were comfortable there, but they missed their mother. The emu business hadn't created any great wealth yet, but Linda told the girls she would send for them as soon as it did. Elizabeth confided to Mary that Fred had checked up on the emu farm. It seemed that Will had pulled out of the project right after the emus arrived. Before he left, he maxed out all of Linda's credit cards and wrote a pile of bad checks. No one knew where he was, and Linda never mentioned Will's disappearance. Elizabeth and Fred were relieved that such a seemingly bad influence was out of the picture. At least, they wouldn't have to worry so much about the girls when they went to visit their mother. Now, their only worry was that one of the emus would attack the girls. Their friends who traveled to Australia had mentioned how dangerous the birds could be.

Over lunch one day, right after Mary had gotten back from vacation, Mary confided to Roxanne that she *had* seen Mark in Hawaii, and that she thought they were going to get together. After days and weeks of no word from the Montana Ranger, Roxanne no longer asked about him. He became something like a receding hairline on a woman that everyone was aware of, but no one wanted to talk about.

Since Mary's problems were too complex to fix over lunch, the two women began to concentrate on Ray's problems. He was in love. Again. This time, he may have gotten lucky. The new guy was an architect Ray met at a cocktail party the magazine gave for its advertisers while Mary was in Hawaii. The man had a loft on the top floor of an old brewery. Ray spent a lot of time there, but Mary and Roxanne couldn't figure out if the man was as smitten with Ray as Ray was with him. Their friend said he was having the time of his life and didn't care where it would go, but the women were worried that flying so high, even inside a loft, could lead to a dangerous fall. Nothing was said to Ray about their concerns. They were fairly sure that if they asked questions, it could put them into the "old biddy" category, and neither one of them wanted to go there.

Meanwhile, Roxanne's relationships were a cause for riotous laughter. It turned out she wasn't kidding about her search for a rich man with a yacht. Every Friday, after work, Mary watched her leave with a detailed plan to find her fantasy man. She approached the project as if she'd won a government grant to find eligible, available men in the upper income bracket. At home, she told her friends, her dining room had been turned into a war room with newspaper clippings taped over the gold-framed mirror, and reference materials strung out all over the walnut table. She scoured the back issues of their magazine for articles about who's who in the Northwest and hung out every weekend at museums, art galleries, trendy bars, and marinas. She showed up to volunteer for boards on all kinds of community projects and was welcomed with open arms when it was discovered she worked for a local magazine. She joked about ordering a tee-shirt emblazoned with "Free Ad Space" on its front.

And she did meet a lot of men. She broke them up into categories: too young, too married, too possessive, too self-centered, too fat, too bald, and those just too stupid to order their own coffee. She said there were a lot of those. The worse were the golfers. Roxanne was on a timetable. She was out for fun and had no time to wait all day for a man who was out playing eighteen holes somewhere. She described golfers as men who wasted a perfectly good sunny day playing a game so they could bore her all through a starry night talking about it. Meanwhile, her want list grew, and that made her search for the right man more difficult. Recently, she'd added good dancer to her list. The week before, she'd added good cook. So far, she hadn't had anything but casual dates, but she was having way too much fun to be discouraged.

Every Monday morning she regaled her two office friends with the results of her hunt for Captain Marvelous. Mary was grateful for the distraction, and all of them laughed when one of the men she'd tried to flirt with was the pilot of a yacht named *Lofty Ideas*. It turned out to be Ray's new love, as he took his cruiser through the locks. Roxanne said she was just about to wave when she saw Ray sit down at the baby grand to play some tunes. Ray said that at least Roxanne was right about one thing: he *was* a *marvelous* captain.

Mary looked wide-eyed at the two of them. "A grand piano? On a yacht?" They both nodded yes. She would have made a joke about Ray striking gold, but one look at the man made it clear he was smitten. Boat, smoat. Ray was in love.

September in the Northwest was glorious as it often was. October moved in gently, it nudged the trees and turned their leaves to gold before they flittered off to dance in cool breezes or float on clear waters like little ships, that bravely set out for far-off lands on ocean currents. Thanksgiving came and went, although not as graciously as it could have. Kate and Mary were invited to Mark's parents' for dinner. Mary only accepted because Kate wanted to go so badly to see her cousins. At first, she planned to drop Kate off and pick her up at the end of the day, but Elizabeth mentioned casually that Mark wouldn't be there. No one ever noticed that Mary had long ago stopped wearing her hibiscus ring. If she were questioned, she planned to say it had turned her finger green.

December turned cold and mean. For Christmas vacation, Kate's cousins went to stay with their mom on the emu farm. Because of a lack of finances, Linda had abandoned plans to fly them back east to spend Christmas with her family. Kate went on a cruise on the new company yacht with her father and his latest girlfriend. Roxanne bravely put on a fur Santa hat and continued her quest for Captain Marvelous, and Mary was determinedly growing a thick turtle shell over her heart. Of the three, Ray was having the best Christmas. In Anthony, he had definitely found a keeper. His new friend seemed to have an open loft 24/7 during the holidays and he often invited Roxanne and Mary. They almost always accepted. His friends topped the list of Seattle's elite, and his parties kept Roxanne and Mary scrambling for something new to wear to each affair. It was fun. Ray didn't have to tell them that not all of his new friends were gay. That was obvious. Roxanne even found a few possibilities for Captain Marvelous. Mary was the only one in the small office who lacked Christmas cheer. The men she met at the parties in Anthony's loft swam around her like salmon swimming around a piece of driftwood. One look at her face and men knew she was more interested in what was on their appetizer plate than she was in them. Ray said that he had someone picked out for Mary, but he had gone to his cabin in Idaho for Christmas. Or was it Montana? He didn't mention a name, and Mary didn't think much about it. She was almost certain that Ray was just trying to cheer her up.

Kate went to her dad's as soon as school was out, leaving Mary with way too much time on her hands. She worked so hard on her stories that she was issues ahead. Most evenings, Roxanne was out interviewing men to be Captain Marvelous, so Mary had the cleanest oven, refrigerator, and closets in the neighborhood. Stubbornly, she put up a small tree. Each holiday, she bought a few ornaments to remember the year's events. This year, she had mixed feelings about her purchases; she'd purchased a decoration made from a seashell, a tiny computer to represent her job, and a little forest ranger she'd bought from a Nisqually Jack's Christmas catalog Ray had at the office. The last ornament tugged at her heart, so she hung it near the bottom of the tree, so it wouldn't be at eye level whenever she came into the room.

She was looking at paint samples for her bedroom when the phone rang. Distracted by color swatches, she didn't look at the caller ID before she answered the phone.

"Mary? It's Mark. Merry Christmas!"

Mary opened her mouth, but no sound came out. She didn't even know what she wanted it to say. *Get lost? Don't get lost? What?*

"Mary, you're not going to hang up on me, are you?"

"Merry Christmas, Mark," Mary said coolly.

Mark was ill at ease. Tentatively, he said, "Hey, look, Mary. The reason I'm calling is that all of the rangers that you met on the beach in Hawaii are coming for Christmas, and I was hoping you'd come too."

Silence.

"They'd love to see you." Mark's voice took on a tone of despair and remorse, "I'd love to see you too."

More silence.

"Mary? Mary, I'm sorry. Please come. You don't even have to worry about getting a ticket. You can ride on the flight that's bringing the rangers over."

"I don't think this is a good idea," Mary finally said. "Kate and I have plans."

"Kate is with her father. I just talked to him. Look, I understand that you're hurt. Maybe we can work this thing out if you come over."

"Mark, I have to go. Merry Christmas." After Mary hung up the phone, she collapsed on the couch and pulled a woolen comforter over her head and sobbed. She cried herself to sleep and hours went by.

When she awoke, it was getting dark outside, and snowflakes were beginning to float past her window. Her tiny Christmas tree was gaily blinking; the reflection from its little white lights bounced off the living room walls and landed on the frosty front yard outside the window. While a fresh pot of coffee perked, she fixed her face, did her hair, and pretended she had someplace to go. She was going for her second cup of coffee when there was a tentative knock on the door. The beat-up old pick-up in her driveway didn't look familiar, but Mary went to the door anyway. Normally, to be safe, she talked to strangers through the living room window that was eight feet off the ground, but how could things get any worse? The way Mary was feeling, she could give any mugger the fight of his life.

"Hi, my name is Jackson," the friendly face with a Santa hat on his head said. "We haven't met, but Mark sent me to pick up his rangers at the airport."

Mary looked at the small truck. There was no way the beach party could fit in that small cab. But who else could know about

Mark's Christmas plans? She opened the storm door and Jackson explained.

"Oh, I don't have them," he said, looking at the truck. "All of their planes got snowed in. The whole west coast is shutting down."

Jackson took out his cell phone and dialed a number. "Mark, she's here." He handed the phone to Mary just as she figured out who Jackson was. His cartoon face was on the cover of the Nisqually catalog. *That* Jackson.

"Mark? What have you done?"

"Mary, pack a few things and fly back with Jackson, will you, please?"

All of a sudden Mary looked at a freezing Jackson, still on her porch, with the first snowflakes of the coming storm sticking to his eyelashes. Quickly, she pulled the man upstairs and pointed him to the big rocking chair by the tree. While she talked to Mark, she pointed to the coffeepot, and Jackson eagerly filled a cup.

Confused, she asked, "How? There are no flights available this close to Christmas."

"He's my friend who has his own plane, and he's a good pilot."

Jackson interrupted. "Mary, I hate to rush you, but our window for takeoff may not be there much longer. We really need to leave now."

Jackson brushed against the Christmas tree and Mary saw the little forest ranger ornament dance up and down. The next thing she knew, she had given the phone back to her new friend and was running down the hall. "Ten minutes. Just give me ten minutes!"

"I'll unplug the tree and coffeepot," Jackson called down the hall. "Should I leave some food out for the cat?"

"No cat," Mary called back. "No dog and no bird, but can you make sure the backdoor is locked?"

"Will do."

Before Mary tore out the door, she went by the tree and grabbed the little forest ranger.

"He's cute, isn't he?" Jackson asked. "He was a sample I had made for Mark by a small company in Canada. He came out so well, we ordered a bunch of them."

"Okay, I know who you are, now, but how close are you to Mark's?"

"We're neighbors. His cabin is about a mile from mine. I'm sorry we had to meet under these rushed circumstances, but we'll get better acquainted on the flight over."

"You said you have a plane? Is it at Sea-Tac?"

"No, it's here at your local field. I borrowed the controller's pickup. He said he'd hold my plane for security," Jackson laughed. "I was headed to Sea-Tac, but when I found out I didn't have any passengers, I called Mark and he asked me to come here. The plane is loaded with snacks I got for the rangers. We'll have a picnic as soon as we take off."

The local airfield wasn't far from Mary's house. She was in the plane's passenger seat and strapped in before she had a chance to be nervous. Air traffic was slow, so they took off right away.

The weather was worsening. Heavy snow was predicted later that night. Jackson checked the weather with the controller, and they both were confident Jackson would make it to Montana before the weather caught up with him. To ease Mary's mind, Jackson assured Mary that his plane was equipped with state of the art de-icing equipment, and if the weather got worse, the plane could handle it.

As soon as they were airborne, Jackson opened up a treasure chest of deli food. He laughed when he saw Mary try to get her mouth around one of the huge sandwiches she'd found in the ice chest. "Sorry that's so big. I told the guy at the deli I was throwing a picnic for big, hungry men." He easily downed a sandwich and a soft drink before Mary had finished half of her sandwich.

"I can't believe you went to all of this trouble for Mark and a bunch of rowdy rangers," Mary said.

"I figured he needed cheering up. He's been moping around since he left you this summer. You know, don't you, that he's been trying to relocate to the west coast? It hasn't been easy. So far, all he's gotten is a lot of no-vacancy replies."

"I didn't know anything about that," a surprised Mary said.

"Well, maybe I shouldn't have said anything. I was sure you knew. He said he couldn't ask you to leave your job at a magazine just to climb trees and chase bears with him all day."

Mary was overcome. With tears in her eyes, she said, "Right now, it's sounding pretty good to me."

Jackson looked at her and relief spread across his face. It was obvious he and Mark were close, and he cared about his friend's happiness. He urged her to take a nap after she'd eaten. He said he'd wake her up in plenty of time to watch the approach into the airfield. You'll see Mark and my cabins when we fly over. If the weather is still good, maybe we'll buzz his place as we come in."

Hours later, Jackson gently shook Mary's shoulder and told her they had just crossed the Montana border. While Mary fixed her hair and face, Jackson called Mark, who was already at the airfield, waiting for them.

"I'm glad to hear your voice," Mark said. "The weather in Seattle is awful. Can Mary hear me?" he asked. Jackson assured him that she could. "Mary, Kate called and wanted you to know that they were safely docked on Orcas Island, and if there were an emergency and they had to come home in the snow, the boat is fully loaded with radar and all the rest of that stuff. She called me because you didn't answer at home. She was worried."

Jackson and Mary looked at each other and cringed. "Remembered the cat, forgot the kid," Mary said, embarrassed. Toward the microphone, she asked, "Does she know where I am?"

"No, I told her that I'd called just as you were leaving with Roxanne in her Hummer for some party. She bought my story."

Jackson's plane flew into the airfield just ahead of the first snow flurry. Mark had driven the park's snowplow to the field in case he needed it, and the three of them piled aboard. The men looked up and predicted that the heavy snow was just an hour or so behind them.

When Jackson settled into the cab of the plow, he commented that he and Mark were a perfect pair. He had the plane and Mark had the snowplow, and it would take both of them to get them to their cabins. The conversation could have been awkward with other men. Instead, the two men caught up on news in and around the park. Jackson's cabin inside the park boundaries had been grandfathered in for years, and new developers were considered encroachers by both men. So far, no park "enrichment" plans had passed. Mark had kept an eye on Jackson's cabin, and it was still locked up tight. The grizzly that had been hanging around had moved on to garbage cans with looser lids.

Mary thanked Jackson when they got to his cabin and gave him a big hug. "You saved my Christmas, Jackson," she told him. The man hurried inside to start a warm fire, and left Mark and Mary alone. That was when it got embarrassing. "I'm not sure if I should be here," Mary hesitantly said.

"I'll make it worth your time," Mark promised with a grin.

"Not so fast, Smokey," Mary said without much conviction.

"Can we fight later? It's been a long time," Mark said as he drew Mary to him.

She murmured, "What are we fighting about? I've forgotten."

When they got to Mark's place, Mary was glad to find a warm cabin with a fire waiting for her. The smell of pine drew her attention to a huge tree in the corner of the cabin that had an antique sleigh parked underneath its boughs. Decked out in red ribbon and filled with gifts, it had obviously been meant for the rangers that were stuck in airports all along the coast.

Mark pulled Mary to him and folded her into his arms. All of Mary's resolve melted away. This was where she wanted to be. Why pretend she could ever feel differently? There, surrounded by the smells of cinnamon, pine, and the crackling fire, they stood together, wrapped in their own celebration of togetherness.

Mark sighed when the phone rang and he saw his mother's name on the caller ID. "It's Mom," he said, with a slight smile. "Hi, Mom. Merry Christmas to you, too." Mary was moving toward the bedroom with her suitcase when she heard Mark's voice change. "Why would I do that? Where are you?" he looked at Mary with a forlorn look. "Here? You're *here*? You mean at the airstrip? I'll be right there."

Mary was panicked, and looked in vain for someplace to hide. "Oh, God. Why?"

"She and Dad didn't want me to be alone at Christmas. Dad flew the twin engine over. I've got to go get them Mary. Do you want to face the music now or later?"

"What *other* choices do I have?" a frustrated Mary asked.

"If you really don't want to see them, I could have Jackson come and pick you up."

Mary groaned, "And then what?"

"I guess you'd have to stay with him, there's no other cabins or lodges up here."

Trapped. She was trapped. Mary threw up her hands. "Mark, this just wasn't meant to be. Please call Jackson. I'll make it up to him somehow."

Not long after, Jackson arrived at Mark's cabin, still wearing the Santa hat and driving a red snow mobile. "Mary, I'm going to get you so drunk on rum toddies you won't even remember tonight," he promised.

Mark took off to pick up his parents. He wasn't totally at ease as he watched Mary climb onto the back of a shiny red snowmobile with the most eligible bachelor in the West. As badly as things were going, there was nothing to say they couldn't get worse. Mark watched Jackson race away across the snow with his Christmas wrapped around his friend's waist until they were out of sight. Sadly, he headed toward the snowplow.

Jackson's cabin looked like the magazine layout it was. He told Mary that they shot the cover for his Christmas catalog there. Everywhere she looked, there were products from Jackson's stores. "This cabin is perfect," she told him.

"Thanks, I liked it so much I bought everything. I've got a dynamite designer on my staff. She did it all. I was hoping she'd come with the design, but she said she had a guy already." His voice was a little sad, and Mary wondered what this other guy must have going for him. He looked so uncomfortable Mary decided she should change the subject.

"Jackson, what would I do without you? Somehow, I'll make this up to you."

"I'm not worried about it. I wasn't doing anything, anyway," he said sadly. "I asked Santa for a girl, but he couldn't deliver. I guess she wasn't in the catalog." He handed Mary a rum toddy, as promised. "This is number one. We've got enough booze laid in to make any ex-mother-in-law begin to look like Tinkerbell."

They were looking through his huge collection of DVDs when the phone rang. With surprise and alarm in his voice he urgently questioned the caller. His forgotten drink sat untouched on the coffee table. There was no question that there was trouble, big trouble, in the Internet catalog sales department. After Jackson finished his call he said, "Mary, you're welcome to stay here as long as you want, but something has come up. I have to fly back to Seattle. There's a problem at the store."

"Fly back? Through the storm?"

"I checked the weather when we got in, and I think the worst of the storm finally went another direction. That's how Mark's parents were able to make it over."

"Jackson! Take me with you! Is that possible? Mark's parents could be here for days, at least until Christmas is over. I feel like such a fool. Please, Jackson!"

"Alright. I'll call Mark and tell him what's going on. Will you lock the backdoor, and unplug the coffeepot?"

"What about the cat?" Mary kidded.

They both laughed as they ran for his snowmobile. On the way, Jackson told Mary he never got to talk to Mark. His mother answered the phone. He left a cryptic message that Mark could easily unravel. He might not like it, but he'd get the picture.

18

A mountain rescue

Before he warmed up the plane, Jackson refueled the tanks and checked the de-icing fluid. While the plane warmed up, he made a thermos of coffee for the trip. The plane hadn't been unloaded, and the food leftover from the trip over was still on board, so they had a second picnic while Jackson piloted them through a canopy of stars brighter than usual due to the clean air left after the storm.

They were both marveling over how beautiful it was when the engine started sputtering. Jackson never stopped chatting, but his voice became serious and, as a precaution, he began to scan the landscape for a place to land. He was about to tell her there was really nothing to worry about when the engine quit altogether. Calmly, Jackson picked up the microphone to the radio and called in a Mayday. Mary, frozen in her seat, said nothing, and did what she was told. "Tighten your seatbelt and hang on. I'm going to try to land us on that patch of snow with no trees on it," Jackson instructed, as he pointed to a snowy patch below them. Mary looked where he pointed. "Mary, listen to me. If anything goes wrong, stay near the plane. We're between Missoula and Spokane; someone will find us soon. There's an ELT—electronic locator transmitter—on the plane that will lead them right to us." Jackson looked at Mary. She was too quiet. "Are you with me?" he asked urgently. Mary nodded. "Now, listen. Everything you need is here on the plane. Food, a first-aid box, flares," he pointed to everything as he spoke. "Use your cell phone if it works. Stay calm." With that, Jackson landed the plane as smoothly as if he were on a runway. "Hey, that was fun. Want to do it again?" he kidded. *What a guy. That girl who turned him down is missing out on a great catch. I hope that, whoever she is, she knows what she's doing.*

After the plane came to a full stop, he nimbly jumped out and started putting emergency flares around the aircraft. From the back of the plane, he pulled out what seemed to be at least one of everything in his catalog. He quickly set up a tent, and dressed it with sleeping bags and lanterns. Mary pleaded to help, but Jackson insisted that things would go a lot faster if he did it, as he was familiar with all of the equipment. When everything was set up to his liking, he climbed back into the plane and poured a cup of coffee for both of them.

"Why can't we stay in the plane?" Mary asked as she looked at the camp Jackson had set up.

"We probably will, but if I begin to smell a gas leak, we'll have to get out fast. This way, our camp is all set up and we won't have all of our survival equipment blowing up with the plane."

"Do you think we have a gas leak?"

"I hope not, but I hit something coming in. I think it was a big rock. Did you call 911?" Jackson asked playfully.

"I tried, but I couldn't get a signal."

"It's getting cold in here. Crawl into the tent and get into a sleeping bag. I'm going to check the plane and see if I can get someone to talk to me on the radio."

Mary turned to get into the tent and stopped. "Jackson, you did a beautiful job," she said to the man as he checked underneath his plane. "I never doubted you for a minute."

Jackson smiled, obviously pleased.

In the tent, both in their sleeping bags, the two chatted about Jackson's business and his computer problem. Jackson also filled Mary in on his family's cabin on the lake, and how much fun he and Mark had fishing from the plane when they landed on the water with the floats on. Mary was hoping to ask him about the girl he was interested in, but the timing was bad. Jackson had enough worries on his plate.

Both of them were still in the tent in down sleeping bags, laughing and finishing the coffee when they heard helicopters overhead.

"That was quick," Jackson said, as he checked his watch, "just under fifty minutes."

He looked up and counted three helicopters, and groaned, "Mary, I've got bad news. Only one of those helicopters is a rescue chopper."

Puzzled, Mary asked, "What do you mean?"

"I mean the other two are from television stations. I can see their call letters from here. Listen to me. If you try to duck the cameras, it'll look like we're trying to hide something. The best thing to do is to smile and wave, like we're at a church picnic."

Mary agreed. She looked up and saw the call letters from the television stations emblazoned on the sides of the helicopters in big, bright letters, and got an insight into what Jackson's life was like. He was famous. The news cameras would be all over them. Most of the feeds would be live, putting the two of them on every channel in every state in the Northwest. Within minutes, while they were still in the air, television cameras were filming Mary and Jackson with only their heads sticking out of their cozy sleeping bags. The newsmen all knew who Jackson was, and wanted to know who was that with him?

On the television screen back in Mark's cabin, the screen on Brian's yacht, the widescreen television in the loft in downtown Seattle where a big party was going on, and on Roxanne's tiny bedroom television, perfectly clear film of Mary and Jackson's mountain rescue surprised and alarmed their friends.

As luck would have it, Mark was left to answer everyone's questions. Even Roxanne called Mark's phone number in Montana.

Mary thought she could hear the phones ringing in every cabin, house, and boat in her address book.

As soon as the helicopters landed, Jackson tried to draw attention away from his passenger by getting out of the tent and moving toward the plane to answer questions, but there were enough cameras to cover both of them. He turned back to Mary, shrugged his shoulders, and mouthed he was sorry. It must have been a slow news night, because the reporters and cameramen used up enough film to make a small documentary, and seemed in no hurry to leave. The next time she spoke to Jackson, they were on the rescue helicopter headed for Spokane where Jackson had arranged to pick up a charter plane. As soon as they got close to civilization, both of their phones started ringing. Mary just let hers go to voicemail. Jackson did the same, except for a call that came in from a girl named Cameron. Mary noticed Jackson answered that call on the first ring.

19
Nice look, kiss me anyway

Mary never heard from Mark, and she was almost relieved. She had no idea he was flying back with his parents in their plane and had an estimated arrival at her house of about four twenty in the morning. Before she went to sleep, she called Kate to assure her she was okay, but she said she was very tired, and could all of the other questions wait until tomorrow? A message from Roxanne on her voicemail simply asked, "What are you doing in a sleeping bag with my Captain Marvelous?" She added that their boss had said for Mary to take the next day off. Completely clueless about Mark's imminent arrival, Mary went to bed in a tee-shirt emblazoned with the North Hill Pet Cemetery logo that Mildred had given her, and a pair of old wool ski socks. A few hours later, she almost didn't hear Mark leaning on her doorbell that chimed *Love Me Tender*.

Mary wasn't fully awake until she looked through the peephole and saw Mark on her doorstep. Even then, she wasn't conscious enough to look down at her sleep attire.

The first thing Mark said to her was, "Are you alright?"

"I'm fine. Jackson is a wonderful pilot, and he's got a great bedside manner. He should be a doctor. I wasn't even frightened."

Relieved, Mark looked down at Mary's tee-shirt. "Nice look. Kiss me anyway."

"How did you get here?" asked a surprised Mary.

"Mom made dad fly us back. She felt so bad about ruining our Christmas and even worse about putting you in danger."

"Oh, no. Your poor father must have been exhausted."

"He was tired, but I sat up front with him all the way and poured coffee down him. Mom slept all the way back," he grinned, "so she was fine. Anyone who thinks Mom doesn't rule the roost should have been there when he tried to put his foot down and tell her we could all go back the first thing in the morning. She was having none of that." Mark began to feel the exhaustion take over him, and he asked, "Can I sleep on your couch? We'll talk in the morning."

"No," Mary answered, "but you can sleep in my bed."

Under Mary's comforter, Mark wrapped his arms around Mary and they both slept. Their path was clear for the first time in months. When the sun was up, they would both put on their snow boots and slog through anyone's denials, protestations, and other seemingly insurmountable details, and get on with their life. After what they'd already been through, it should be easy.

Mary heard the water in the shower running the next morning at the same moment she remembered that Mark was with her. The night before, when she was in a plane that made a forced landing that resulted in her face being splashed across every television screen in four states, seemed unreal. She put on a pot of coffee and waited for the show to begin.

The first thing Mark said when he got out of the shower was, "Mary, marry me. Now."

"Okay! Can we skip the church and engraved invitations?"

"Good idea. I don't want anything to slow us down. What about Kate?"

"If she's in the marina, we can pick her up on the way. If not, we can explain it to her over the phone. Do we have a number for your girls?"

"No, I'll have to call Mom. I don't think they can fly back. Linda would have a fit."

Mark turned sideways so Mary could reach the coffeepot. He commented, "If our girls were here, we'd be in total gridlock."

The two moved into the living room and plugged in the Christmas tree lights while they drank their coffee. Dreamily, Mary leaned back against the sofa and took in the smells. The tree, fragrant and green. The fresh, manly smell of Mark, and the spicy smell of the coffee, a special Christmas blend from Roxanne. Mark got up to spread an afghan from the couch and a few pillows in front of the tree and gently guided Mary to a bed made for two people caught up in the joy of the season. The phone rang somewhere off in the distance, unable to reach two lovers who were celebrating the blissful conclusion of an improbable union with a never-ending future.

When they got around to the phone messages, there were a lot of them.

Kate wanted a call back. When they returned her call, they learned the yacht was still in the marina at Orcas Island. She hated to miss the wedding, but she was fully supportive of them marrying right away.

Mary asked if she was having a good time, and Kate told her that her dad's date was not much older than she was and a lot of fun.

Brian got on the line. What was Mark thinking, he wanted to know? What was he doing shacking up with his ex-wife? Mark just shook his head and hung up on him.

Mark's parents wanted them to drop over for a "talk". Mark called his mother and explained that he and Mary were tying up loose ends and that they'd see them after Christmas.

There was a call from Jackson, checking to see if Mark made it to Mary's all right. He also mentioned that the plane was fixed. It was a minor problem with a fuel line; there was no other damage. He was flying back to his cabin and would be glad to give them a lift if they were interested. Yes! Mark called him back right away and made arrangements for Jackson to pick them up on his way. The strangest call of all was from Linda, who said she knew where Mary had been, and just how long had her affair with Mark been going on? How could they do that to the girls? Do *what*? The two wondered. They deleted the call.

When they made a quick dash to the county building to get a license, they discovered the building was closed, due to a combination of bad weather and the holiday. They would have to wait to get married. It was just as well; it would give them time to get the girls together. Mark had an uneasy feeling that the small, quick wedding that they wanted had the potential to get out of hand, but Mary didn't seem to be worried. She kept telling him that he had to have more faith in her and Roxanne's planning skills.

"Roxanne is coming?" he pretended shock.

At the airport, Mark and Mary parked her car right next to the truck that Jackson had borrowed to pick her up the first time. They ducked inside to get permission to leave the car there for a few days. It was no problem. Any friend of Jackson's was a friend of his, the man said. Mary noticed a gigantic can of Nisqually popped caramel corn on the counter with a big red bow on the lid, obviously sent from Jackson. On the bulletin board behind the counter, was a snap of the man with his new friend, obviously taken the first time Jackson had borrowed the man's truck. The personable catalog man looked right at home with the other photos on the bulletin board of men with their giant salmon, kids in overalls, and proud pilots with their planes.

Right on time, Jackson made a beautiful landing, and scooped the two up. To Mary, it was almost like an eagle swooping over a lake, snagging a fish in its sharp talons without ever slowing down or breaking rhythm.

She hardly got to speak as the two friends quickly recapped the last few days. Jackson filled Mark in on the glitch in the computer system for the Internet catalog. "I really know nothing about computers," he laughed, "but I know the people who do, and Christmas is no time to tick-off customers."

"Did you get it fixed?" Mark asked.

"Oh, sure, eventually. But half the catalog department was there when our plane went down, and when they saw me and Mary on television, they used our email system and alerted the whole company. By the time I got there, the whole office building was lit up and everyone was hanging around waiting for news. When I walked in, they started to party. Most of us were up all night." Mark said something that Mary couldn't hear, and Jackson just shook his head sadly and shrugged. It was something about Cameron, the woman Jackson had a phone call from when they were in the helicopter. From what she understood, she hadn't been in town and he hadn't seen her.

Mark told Jackson about the new navigational equipment his dad had installed on his twin engine. Jackson was quick to approve, telling Mark that it was smart to get the top of the line if you were flying over mountains. The two laughed that they could all save a lot of money if they moved to a flatter state.

The small talk didn't hide the fact that they were both anxious to get back to the Christmases they'd originally planned. It was a beautiful flight, and the men laughed when the snowplow started right up without any coaxing. "It's a good omen, Mark. Maybe nothing else will go wrong for the rest of the holidays. I'm going back next week. Let me know if you want a ride, Mary."

"Oh, my gosh! I forgot all about work! I'd better call my boss and let her know I'll be gone for a few days."

"Will that be a problem?" Mark asked.

"No, it's slow right now. We just put out an issue. My vacation is used up, so they'll just not pay me for the days I'm not there."

Jackson commented that at least they'd remembered the cat. It was becoming their private joke. Mark was clueless, and Mary promised to explain later.

They dropped Jackson off in much the same way he had picked them up at the airport. Mark kidded, "Jackson, I'm going to slow down, and I want you to open the door, and tuck and roll."

Suddenly, Jackson shouted and his face lit up. A car was parked outside his cabin, and a very cold woman was bundled up in the front seat. Jackson was out of the snowplow before it fully stopped. Mark asked why Cameron hadn't flown over with them, and Jackson explained that she'd been doing some work at the store in Idaho. Mark didn't wait around for introductions. There'd be time for that over the next week or so. Mary turned her head and watched the two as they headed for the cabin door. She had no idea what had changed the woman's mind, but Jackson was obviously thrilled. Even Mark couldn't stop grinning. Apparently, Jackson had told him all about the catalog designer.

Mark slowed down at the mailbox and hesitated before he pulled it open. Mary could have sworn he held his breath. All he found was a stack of magazines and assorted junk mail. Nothing looked as if it could be a job offer. She could tell he was unhappy, but he said nothing.

To hide his disappointment, he chatted about the cabin. "This is our front yard. It's under three feet of low-maintenance snow right now. In the summer, it's mostly barked flowerbeds with more bark than flowers. I'm not much of a gardener. If a tourist mentions the lack of landscaping, I tell them we're conserving water. They never mention the lake a few feet away." He pulled her through the living room, kitchen, and bathroom with the speed of a needle passing through cranberries. "This is where we'll sleep—sometimes," he said as he drew her into the bedroom.

Mary had never imagined what his bedroom might look like, and she was delighted with the rustic bed that still had bark on its frame, and the Hudson's Bay blanket in white with broad colorful stripes at each end. Above the bed, there was a framed print of Indians on The Trail of Tears. One of them was wearing a blanket over his shoulders, just like the one on the bed.

"I love this, and it smells like fresh cut wood," Mary said. "You didn't make it, did you?"

"No," Mark said regretfully, "I'm not that handy. I got it out of Jackson's catalog, but I did assemble it. It came with instructions in three different languages. The ones in Japanese were the easiest to understand."

"Well, it's beautiful, but Mark, where were you going to put all of those visiting rangers?"

"I have a bunkhouse in the administrative building. We use it for firefighters and conferences. It's bare bones with no privacy, but the people who come here like it. They also like the price. It's free." Mark was turning to leave the bedroom when he stopped and blurted, "Mary, I'm applying for work with the Washington Parks Department. I know you'd never be happy here without a job."

"Not so fast, Smokey. I'm a writer, I can work anywhere. If not for the magazine, for someone else. Or I could freelance. Our problem is Kate. I'd hate to uproot her in her senior year. Could we wait until school is out before we move over here?" A surprised Mark was speechless. All he could do was hold out his arms and wrap them gratefully around Mary.

"Although I might have to give up the ad-selling part of my job," Mary kidded, "I have never had a sales pitch that worked on bears."

Mark was surprised and relieved, "I never expected you to be so flexible."

Mary barely heard him. She was already planning to sell her house after Kate graduated from high school in June. Then they could move all of their girls to the park. His girls loved it there, and had been upset when their mother had moved them to the coast where her opportunities to party and meet men were more abundant. There was little doubt that they would welcome the move.

For now, they had the cabin to themselves. Quietly, Mark took Mary's hand and led her to the bed. Outside, snow was beginning to fall. It was a thick, heavy snow that clung to the trees and hugged the roof of the cabin. The next day was Christmas. It didn't bother him at all to know they could easily be snowed in until after New Year's.

Mark had ordered a delicate, gold chain bracelet for Mary, but she'd never had a chance to shop, so Christmas morning, they made a pot of coffee and opened the gag gifts Mark had purchased for the visiting rangers. When Mary opened a package of x-rated, temporary tattoos, she insisted Mark try them out. Her favorite was The Big Kahuna. It really was big.

Park 101

During the next few days, Mark took Mary with him everywhere. She learned how to start the snowplow, clear the runway, run the radios, and read the map of the park. Mark showed her how to find any information she might need during an emergency. That included where the list was for the search and rescue volunteers, how to run the emergency generator, and how to read the weather reports. "The girls will help you when they get here," he promised, "they know it all. But if something happens before then, I want you to know where things are." The last thing he showed her was where the key was hidden for the gun cabinet. "Bears haven't been a problem for years, but Jackson did have a bear trying to get into his garbage recently. You'll need to know how to fire a rifle if there's ever a problem and I'm not around. We'll do some target practicing."

"I'd hate to have to shoot one of those magnificent creatures," Mary answered.

"Oh, believe me," Mark said, "you won't have any trouble shooting one if you feel you or the girls are threatened." Then, he kidded, "if you ever have to shoot one, make it a clean shot and we'll make a rug for the bedroom."

After the holidays, Mark drove Mary home, then turned around and drove back to Montana because Jackson told everyone at the home office he was snowed in, and may not be able to get out for weeks. Coincidentally, Cameron had called in sick. No one was fooled. Everyday, his secretary peeked into his empty office and giggled, then the laughter spread to the rest of the floor. Their boss was happy and so were they. His secretary, a woman who wore her 30-year pin over her heart, ran the store so well that many people they did business with didn't even realize Jackson wasn't there. He knew she would.

Mark was glad to see his girls, but his closeness to his family made it clear that Brian and Linda were on a mission to break up the romance that strangely threatened them. Mark and Mary puzzled over the phone calls and email messages they received from the two. *Why should they care?*

* * *

Brian even went so far as to try to turn his mother against Mary, claiming that his ex-wife had played around long before *he* ever did.

Elizabeth told Mary that she'd thrown him out. Things hadn't been friendly between them anyway, since he'd sold her yacht without telling her.

Several times a week, she told Mary, she drove by the marina to see the yacht and find out if anyone had bought it yet. Sometimes, she'd park in the marina; she confided she always ended up sobbing. The yacht was sold. It had to be. There was no "For Sale" sign on it.

The small yacht, she said, was a part of her and Fred's history. She'd lost her virginity on that boat with Fred. They'd had it when they'd started their business, raised their boys, and built their first home. On it, the boys had caught their first fish. With that boat, they'd rescued two young girls, inexperienced at scuba diving, who'd been swept far from shore by strong currents. Elizabeth had been convinced God had put Fred and her there at that time, because they had never boated there before. It happened when, one morning, she woke up, pointed to a spot on a map, and told Fred they were going there.

"Why?" Fred had asked.

"I don't know," Elizabeth answered, "but we might as well take a picnic." When they arrived at the spot Elizabeth had chosen, there wasn't another boat in sight for miles. They had just finished their lunch and Fred, who failed to see the appeal of the spot his wife had chosen for lunch, was getting restless to go. That was when they heard girls calling for help. At first, they thought they were hearing birds. Then, Elizabeth told Mary, she could barely make out two heads struggling to stay above water. They were big girls, and their gear was cumbersome; Fred had been unable to bring them aboard. The two boaters towed the girls to shore on a rope. Embarrassed, the girls quickly disappeared up the beach, in the direction of their car, never to be seen again by their rescuers. Elizabeth had never forgotten those girls.

So young.

So beautiful.

So almost dead.

Saved by their little yacht, floating on unfamiliar water on a gray day on Puget Sound, without another soul around for miles.

So much history. So much love. So much life. How could her son have been so cold-hearted?

One time, when she was parked in the marina's parking lot, she saw men working on the boat's interior, and she thought the new owners were updating the yacht to get it ready for the opening day of yachting season. She was determined to wait until she thought it was finished, then walk down the dock to try to get a peek inside. Mary promised to go with her.

After a few cocktails after dinner one night, Fred confided to Mary that he had purchased the yacht the day after his son had sold it, and was having it redone as a surprise anniversary present for Elizabeth. An admission to his wife that the yacht was still theirs would have spoiled the surprise and lightened the pressure on his son. He was in no mood to do either. He was as angry about the swift sale of the family yacht as Elizabeth, and his intention was to let his son twist in the wind as long as possible. Meanwhile, he took measures to insure that he and Elizabeth would remain in charge of their company. He moved all of the financial paperwork and all of the titles to the company's assets to his own personal safe and stopped payment on the new yacht that Brian had christened *Cash me out,* a reference to his trips to the casinos. Before long, Brian would begin to get phone calls from his bank and creditors. Fred couldn't wait for the ship to hit the fan. After the trouble Brian had given Mary and Mark, she had no trouble keeping his secret.

21

Mary figures it out

Meanwhile, Mark and Mary watched Brian and Linda grow in closeness. Oh, it wasn't a romantic arrangement. It was more like two polar bears, adrift at sea, sharing a small piece of ice. After one of their ugly phone calls or emails, Mark would wonder why they were so vindictive. "I know they don't want us back," he'd laugh.

Some of the ugliness began to wash over onto Mark's girls when Linda tried to turn them against their father and Mary. When Karen's asthma started to act up, Mark began to throw socks and underwear into a gym bag with the intention of driving to Linda's emu ranch and rubbing her face into a big pile of emu poo. Before he got out the front door, the phone rang. It was his mother.

"Mom, don't worry, I'm on the way to take care of the problem," he told her.

"Oh, I wouldn't do that," Elizabeth said, with a smile, "her living room is small and it might get crowded. I've sent two of our attorneys over with some paperwork that says that if she doesn't knock it off, she'll need a babysitter for those big chickens of hers. The bank still has her signature on that withdrawal slip, you know, and even though no one knows where Will is now, his is on there too. We can find him if we have to."

"Mom, I'm not sure if you should have gone to the trouble."

"What I'm hearing is that you don't think I should have interfered, but I said nothing until my granddaughters began to suffer. I'm responsible for those girls while they're with me."

Mark had to agree. Besides, not many people won a battle with his mother; he'd learned that much from his father. Before she hung up, she promised to let Mark know what happened as soon as she heard from the attorneys.

Mary and Kate were spending a lot of time at the girls' grandparents', and the cousins were delighted when Elizabeth gave them the keys to Mark's house that they quickly turned into a clubhouse. Mary began to see the playful side of Elizabeth, and the two became close. She wondered if it was Brian's fault they'd gotten off on the wrong foot when they were first married. She remembered that he always put an unpleasant twist on comments about his mother. After years of thinking she didn't fit in, she finally figured it out: it was *Brian* who didn't fit in.

Finally, through emails, Mark and Mary realized that Brian was being nasty because, after he'd purchased the new yacht over his parents' objections, he was worried about his part of his parents' inheritance someday. He had lots of plans for that money; he didn't want to be cheated out of it. Linda had no claim to any family money because she and Mark were divorced, so he convinced her that somehow she was being cheated too.

Mary kept her promise to Fred and didn't mention to Mark that his father had stopped payment on the new yacht. She knew his father would tell Mark when he was ready. She wondered what Brian was going to do. There was no way he had enough credit to put the yacht in his name. How long would it be before it was repossessed?

For Linda's part, maybe some of her ugliness was triggered by her problems with giant chickens. The attorneys reported that, of the four, two of the emus had died, and one hadn't been seen for weeks; it, too, was probably dead. The carcasses were out there, somewhere, buried in the snow, waiting for the spring thaw. Linda had no idea how she was going to dispose of the huge birds. Moreover, bills came in almost daily for supplies that Will had purchased for the ranch before he disappeared. Every week, incubators, heat lamps, feed, and vaccines arrived in the mail with their accompanying bills. It seemed Will had put everything on auto-delivery. Linda had tried to stop the orders, but they kept coming. While the attorneys were there, Linda broke down and admitted that she had no idea how to vaccinate emus or take care of the egg if she ever got one. Will was supposed to take care of raising the birds. The attorneys sympathized with her predicament, but before they left, they saw to it that Linda had signed documents promising that she would refrain from causing anymore problems.

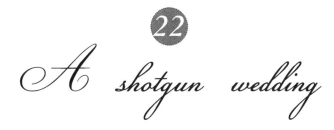

A shotgun wedding

Finally, Mary and Mark began to relax about Linda. Brian wasn't worth their worrying, Mark told Mary. Whatever trouble he was in wasn't their concern. Mark was driving back for his parent's fiftieth wedding anniversary that was coming up, but he had no plans to confront Brian about his behavior. He just hoped his brother showed up. Whatever problems he and his parents had could be put aside for one day.

Apparently, it was an especially dressy affair since they were going to renew their vows. Mary had his father call him twice to remind him to be sure and bring his best suit. He couldn't figure out why everyone seemed to be so worried about what he was going to wear. How could he have guessed that Mary and Elizabeth were throwing a surprise wedding for the two of them right after Elizabeth and Fred renewed their vows? No one could remember ever being invited to a wedding where the groom didn't know he was getting married. The whole idea was reminiscent of the shotgun weddings in the Old West.

The double wedding was Elizabeth's idea. Things had gotten a little out of hand. The ceremony was going to be held at their home and, for weeks, she had been redecorating the house, inside and out, for a guest list that became so long it was embarrassing.

Landscaping was redone outside, a new deck built, and a state-of-the-art, outdoor stainless steel kitchen had been added. The event was going to be catered, so Elizabeth had to confess to Fred that the trendy kitchen on the expanded deck was his anniversary gift. Inside, an interior designer had freshened up the whole house, painted the walls, updated the draperies, and added a strategically-placed window that showcased the upscale landscaping outside.

When Elizabeth questioned Mary about her and Mark's wedding plans one day, Mary had to admit that there were none, except that she and Mark wanted to have a quiet wedding without a lot of fuss. After all, it was a second wedding for both of them, and hardly an occasion for a white dress and all of the trimmings.

"Nonsense!" Elizabeth insisted, "I have an idea! Let's have a double wedding! All the work is done, and we might as well get as much use out of the thousands I've spent as we can. And you've helped so much with this Mary. Let's do it!"

"I don't know," Mary hesitated, "Mark might feel like he's been shanghaied. He definitely wants a small wedding."

"Mary, you deserve more. My first son treated you so badly I've wanted to throw him off that yacht he bought without our permission," Elizabeth said. "I can promise you that Mark will never behave as badly as Brian," she added. Elizabeth saw doubts about her idea in Mary's eyes, so she added, "Besides, I ordered a huge cake. Fred is going to flip when he sees how big it is. I'm afraid I got carried away." They both laughed when they looked over and saw the sketches the caterer had left of the cake. It really was gigantic.

During all of this, Fred was strangely quiet and agreeable. All of the plans for the anniversary allowed him to slip out daily to supervise the finishing touches on Elizabeth's yacht. The interior of the pleasure craft was being re-designed by the same woman Elizabeth had picked to give the house a facelift, so Fred was sure his bride would love the results.

The day of the wedding, Mark pulled into the driveway and gave a low whistle. The whole yard had been re-landscaped. His mother had gone all out, and he hoped that having the house fixed up would take some of the sting out of losing her yacht.

Mary had told him about all of his mother's tasteful decorations and the huge guest list. He was a little sad he couldn't give Mary something as nice. He was early, so he caught Mary by surprise. She never got a chance to break the news about their getting married right after his parents exchanged their vows. The first thing he saw when he went past his bedroom on his way to check the pool's water was Mary's soft, pink dress spread out on the bed. It was not the kind of dress a woman wore *to* a wedding. It was the kind of dress a woman wore to be *in* a wedding. Even a ranger from Montana knew that much. Layers and layers of sheer fabric moved in the breeze from the open window until Mark thought the dress might get up off the bed and dance without Mary in it.

Carefully, Mark backed out of the house and made a noisy entrance into his parents' front door. The first thing he did when he found everyone at the kitchen table was look in the kitchen cupboards. At the coffeepot, he looked in the nearby broom closet. For what, no one knew. When Amy handed him a plate of scrambled eggs and ham, he looked under the table before he sat down.

"What are you looking for?" his mother finally asked.

"Nothing," Mark said with a twinkle in his eye as he savored his breakfast and coffee. When his plate was empty, and he'd drained his second cup of coffee, he asked, "Mary, can I see you outside?"

Mary and Elizabeth's eyebrows raised, and the girls collapsed in laughter. He must have seen the cake with Mary's and Mark's names below his parents', they all thought.

Mark pulled Mary around the side of the house underneath the new ginko tree. "Maaarrry, what have you done?" he asked after he'd pulled her close for a kiss.

"Oh," Mary guessed, "you saw the cake."

"No," Mark answered, "I saw the dress. The one on our bed." Then he asked, "*What* cake?"

They both looked up and saw everyone looking at them from the new window Elizabeth had added to the house so she could see the ginko tree the landscapers had planted. Before Mary could explain, Mark's father was standing there with his arm around Mark's shoulder.

"Congratulations on your wedding day, son!"

"*That's* why you were so worried about my bringing my best suit," Mark laughed, "I kept wondering if you were afraid I might show up for your wedding in my ranger uniform," he said to his dad.

Back inside, his mother asked, "What were you looking for when you came into the kitchen?"

"Oh, I'd already been over to my house, saw Mary's dress, and thought you guys were planning a shotgun wedding. I was looking for a gun!"

Mark never thought he'd be getting married that day, but he had to admire the sentimentality and practicality of the plan. To be sure, it would make the sleeping arrangements for the weekend a lot more fun. Mary had mentioned once that she'd like to sleep in his house so she could get up in the middle of the night and take a nude swim. Tonight might be her night.

On the way back over to Mark's house, Mary filled him in on the guest list. Jackson had known about the surprise from the beginning. "He and Cameron are on their way."

Mark's phone rang. "Mark, where are you?" Jackson asked.

I just got to Mom and Dad's. You gotta suit? Wanna marry Cameron? I hear there's room for your names on the cake."

"Do I have to bring my own shotgun?"

The two laughed over the idea of the double wedding. Mark was as delighted as Jackson thought he'd be.

"Hey, Pal," Jackson said, "I hate to mention this, but when we left, Linda was prowling around your place, looking through the windows. Does she still have a key?"

"No, I changed the locks ages ago. I wonder what she wanted?"

"Maybe she lost one of her emus. Cameron and I talked to her when we drove by, but she didn't say much. She left as soon as she realized she'd been spotted. Cameron was sure she could smell liquor on her breath."

23
Montana Luau

Even Linda didn't know why she was snooping around Mark's cabin, or what she wanted. She had lost everything on her great emu adventure, and she didn't even know anymore if she was running from her creditors, the law, the emus, or all of the above. Will's reckless spending had pushed her way over her credit card limits. She had one emu left, that she knew of, and it was so dangerous she couldn't get near it. It had become very territorial, and attacked Linda whenever she got near her front porch. Linda had crawled into a back kitchen window of her house to get her purse and car keys so she could escape from the feathered beast. Once she got to her car, she started driving and never looked back. The damn emu could have the house and the whole damn ranch. If it couldn't get into the kitchen through the window, it would freeze to death when it got cold. Not that she cared. It would serve it right.

With no extra clothes, no food, and over-maxed credit cards, she lived off the only credit card that had any room on it, her Cart's gas card. She ate all of her meals from the Cart's Pump and Wash stations, bought her cigarettes there, and filled up her tank with gas. If Cart's didn't have it, she didn't get it.

She was pushed to the edge, and the phone call from Brian that morning that told her about Mark's surprise wedding pushed her the rest of the way over. The two had been divorced for years, there was no reason she should care, and really, she didn't. It was just that everyone was getting a new start but her. Fred and Elizabeth were starting over. Brian was starting over with a new yacht and the cheerleader of the week. Mark and Mary were starting over, even her *kids* were starting over. *Where was her fresh start?* She trembled when she realized that she might get her fresh start at Purdy, the women's state prison. That thought was too frightening for her to dwell on. Her mind went back to the weddings. Maybe she'd go over there and crash the ceremonies. Her girls would be there. Brian would be there. Maybe she could be his date. As she drove, she picked up the cell phone to call him, but the call wouldn't go through. Her phone service had been cut off. *Could she get a new, disposable phone at Cart's?* Meanwhile, she opened another screw top bottle of Cart's Cabernet, pointed her car toward the giant wedding cake, and drove.

The big house that belonged to Mark's parents began to fill up early. It was a beautiful day to be on the water, and it was a small community, so a lot of the guests knew about the wedding surprises. The early crowd made it easy for Mark to avoid his brother, who burst through his parents' front door with five Arabs in tow, all of them wearing their traditional clothing with gems that dripped from every finger.

Brian immediately began to drink heavily from the champagne fountain upon arrival, and left his new friends, who spoke little English, to introduce themselves to the other guests. Mark was relieved when Mary told him that Jackson, and not his brother, had been asked to stand by his side. Roxanne said she would stand by Mary, because she wanted to get a closer look at the man who had finally gotten Mary to do a sleepover, even if it was in a sleeping bag.

When Linda arrived, there were no parking spots left at her ex-in-law's house, so she parked in front of Mark's. She wandered through the house, enduring flashback after flashback of her past life. Looking back, she realized it had been pretty good. Mark had been an affectionate husband and a passionate lover. If only he had money; he would have been perfect.

When she passed the bathroom, she got a glimpse of herself in the bathroom mirror; she didn't like what she saw. Despondent and exhausted, she took what was left of the bottle of wine out to the pool, sat down, stuck her feet into the water and cried.

That was where Mary found her when she ran back to the house to get another roll of film. "Linda? What are you doing here?" Mary asked softly when she saw the crumpled and inebriated woman leaning over to look into the water.

"I don't know," Linda admitted, "first, I got a nasty phone call from a collector, then I lost my power, and my emu bit me. Then, I just remember driving."

"Come over and get something to eat."

"Like this? I don't think so."

"Look, I've got some clothes over here. Hop through the shower, put on something of mine, anything you want, and come over." To sweeten the pot, she added, "We've got Arabs. *Rich* ones."

As soon as she got back to the main house, she grabbed Karen and Amy and sent them over to keep an eye on their mom. She was worried that Linda would change her mind, grab what was left of her wine, and hit the freeway. The girls were thrilled about seeing their mother, and rushed right over.

Both of the ceremonies were quick. Elizabeth and Fred both looked wonderful. Her dress was a shorter, more casual version of her wedding gown. Fred couldn't stop grinning and Elizabeth was totally clueless as to why. The more she looked at him, the more his eyes twinkled, until she began to look around the room for the source of his joy. She searched each face for clues, but found only friends and family she and Fred had known for years. None of them were a surprise. She finally decided he was just enjoying the occasion.

Mark and Mary were next in line, and the girls gasped in surprise when Mark slipped the hibiscus ring on Mary's finger. It hadn't turned green!

As soon as the vows were said, Linda zeroed in on the Arabs, and the last Mary saw of her, she was headed toward the beach with one of them. She had no idea she'd picked the dress Mary had worn on the beach with Mark in Hawaii. It hadn't brought Mary much luck that night. Maybe Linda would do better with it. So far, she was off to a good start.

When the time was right, Fred ushered his bride and all of the guests out to the dock, where more champagne was poured. Elizabeth was perturbed that Fred took everyone to the one part of their yard that hadn't been touched by the magic of her landscaper. Twice, she tried to shoo everyone back to their new deck off the kitchen, but no one wanted to go. Elizabeth was puzzled beyond words. About dusk, the little yacht that Elizabeth thought was lost to her forever motored into their slip at the end of their yard. Covered in crepe paper streamers, balloons, and a big "Happy Anniversary" sign, it drew the crowd to the edge of the dock for a better look.

Completely refurbished, the little yacht even had a new name, *After all these years.* The crowd cheered as Fred led Elizabeth through the crowd and onto the little yacht that floated on the water like a toy. The two disappeared inside, and soon, Mark untied the yacht and it headed toward the sound. The celebrators waved and moved back to the house to continue the party.

Brian was first in line for the champagne fountain, or had he ever left? Soon, another boat entered the slip. This one was much smaller, more suited for a lake than the ocean. It, too, was festooned with streamers, balloons, and signs that said "Mary and Mark". Once again, everyone went to the slip, this time to admire the newlyweds' wedding present from Fred. He hadn't told Elizabeth about it for fear of ruining his main surprise, Elizabeth's yacht. The boat was named *Montana Luau,* and Fred had the salesman put a big Smokey Bear on the deck, wearing a silk lei and playing a ukulele.

Linda missed both boats. She worked fast when she got her rich Arab on the beach. No one saw much of her after that. Here, at last, was her fresh start. Within days, she announced to her girls that she planned to marry the sheik in the silk *keffiyeh* and move to Arabia. She'd send for them as soon as she could. No one seriously thought they'd ever see or hear from her again until she changed her mind and wanted to come home. There was never any question that, when that day came, it would probably be the Bergstroms who paid the tab to bring her back. There was no way they could leave the girls' mother in a foreign country if she didn't want to stay, but the family silently agreed that there was also no way the girls would ever be allowed to visit their mother in Arabia. They had never trusted her when she was just on the other side of the mountains.

Meanwhile, there was a story on the news from Okanogan about an emu that had taken over an abandoned house, terrified the local realtors, and chased away the postmen who tried to deliver bills. Several bites had been reported.

Epilogue

For weeks after he and Mary were married, Mark offered the leftover wedding cake that took up a whole shelf in his mother's freezer to Jackson and Cameron. It became such a joke that Mary was afraid Jackson would actually try to use it. She, Elizabeth, and Cameron devised plan after plan of how to get rid of the leftover cake that wasn't aging well because it had a custard filling. Most of the schemes involved dynamite of some kind. In the end, the two lovebirds opted to get married in Hawaii, so Elizabeth and Mary shoveled it into a wheel barrel, rolled it to the dock, and fed it to the seagulls, bite by bite.

The girls moved back to Montana when school was out. As Mark had predicted, it was crowded when they were all together, and The *Montana Luau* became a welcome romantic refuge of Mark and Mary in the summer. One day, when Mark showed up at the boat with matching sheets, a comforter, and matching pillow shams for the sleeping cuddy, Mary was overwhelmed. Before they went into the cabin, Mary winked and said, "Come below…if you dare. I plan to have my way with you."

Mark was intrigued and didn't hesitate.

14902011R00094

Made in the USA
Charleston, SC
07 October 2012